Wyldblood

Issue 8 - Spring 2022

In this issue:

Editorial

Mark Bilsborough

It's going to be hard not to talk about what's going on in the world at the moment so I'm not going to try. I've got a copy of Francis Fukuama's *The End of History* on my shelf and while I applaud the sentiment, reality keeps hitting us squarely in the face. His thesis was that following the Cold War liberal democracy had essentially become the 'end point in mankind's ideological evolution'. Well, maybe that was one step forward and fifteen steps back. He was writing two years before 9/11 and if that didn't upend things Russia's invasion of Ukraine is a forceful reminder that history in all its gory reality is very much alive and kicking.

There was a thriving SFF community in Ukraine before the Russian's 'special military operation' – and I hope there still is. Locus Magazine ran a piece on Ukrainian SF back in 2018 and it's worth a look: https://locusmag.com/2018/01/sf-in-ukraine-by-michael-burianyk/. The article steers us to check out Maryna and Sergiy Dyachenko, H.L Odie, Oleh Shynkarenko and Volodymyr Vynnechenko, and we will. Let's hope they're all safe and well.

No doubt we'll be reading plenty of fiction based on the Ukraine conflict in years to come. Chillingly, plenty of recent SF writers from the region were writing rather presciently about it before it happened – ex-Soviet military officer Fedor Berezin's novels *'War 2010: The Ukrainian Front'* and *'War 2011: Against NATO'* seemingly only got the dates wrong (though the narrative's pro-Russian leanings sit uneasily today), and Andrei Valentinov's *Omega* gives us an occupied Crimea. Predictably, the stories play out in blood and sacrifice.

So it's an uneasy world we find ourselves in, still constrained and battered by COVID and now with the reanimated corpse of the nuclear threat hanging over us. Was Putin serious or just sabre rattling? Certainly the West is nervous enough not to risk committing troops and planes directly to Ukraine. Maybe the apocalypse is now closer than we think.

Military SF has been on the decline in recent years but I'd expect to see a resurgence as our minds focus on conflict. I've never been a fan – too jingoistic, generally, often too violent and too ready to view armed conflict as an objective rather than something to be avoided. But masterpieces like Joe Haldeman's *Forever War* and Orson Scott Card's *Ender's Game* can offer a thoughtful narrative, and John Scalzi's *Old Man's War* series is genuinely entertaining. And then there's *Starship Troopers*, Robert Heinlein's story about a soldier in a war no one understands, killing bug eyed aliens that no-one's bothered to talk to, just following orders. Glorification or condemnation?

Meanwhile stories about peace and reconciliation can give us great happy endings, And we need a happy ending.

Our next issue will be out on July 20th and you'll be able to preorder through the website soon. You can also find us on Amazon (and many other places) which can be a good way to save on shipping outside the UK. Enjoy the stories,

Trees in the Dark

Jordan Chase-Young

The bloated corpse on the concrete sewage bank jerked as Eli tore off his boots. In the ten years that Eli and Spud and Dorian had been hoofing the dead the stench never bothered them. You got used to it in the Guts, where everything lived and ate and shat and died next to one sewage canal or another.

The boys were chanting as they looted the corpse:

O thief in the dark
Take my clothes
Take my bones
But leave my eyes for the rats
And leave my blood for the stones
O thief in the dark

Eli's younger brother Spud, as pimply as his namesake, nudged the corpse's taut head with his fire poker. "Stupid song, really."

"Only cuz it says what you are," said Dorian. "A thief, like us." A pale and gangly sixteen-year-old, he was scouring the dead man's pockets by the light of a burning oil drum. The boys had found just one wallet in their eight years of hoofing, but it was a luxe antique in the Guts, where folks' notion of money was buttons and gum sticks and cigarettes. "But ripejohns don't care if you filch 'em. What's a dead man need with shoes and smokes?"

Crone Maugriss always said to respect the dead, but Dorian had no patience for Crones. To him they were just witches who'd descended from the Great City to rule the children of the underground against their will. Eli felt different; he was sure the children would've cut each other's throats long ago without the Crones to watch over them.

"What's this?" Spud stabbed inside a ripejohn's boot with his fire poker and lifted a fold of yellowed paper.

Eli snatched the paper. "It's got a number. 4060-73G. That sector ain't far, I don't think."

"What's on the back?"

"'Trees,' it says. 'I seen them but the way in's too small. Must find a child to crawl through.'" He looked at Dorian.

The older boy shrugged. "Ramblings."

"Maybe not," said Eli. "*Way in*, like a passage or hideaway. Could be a stash inside, shoes sturdy enough to buy a month of bread."

Dorian scoffed. "Ain't no trees anymore. Not in the whole fucking world. If there was they'd be on the surface, not here."

"You don't know that. You're scared of looking is all."

The boys never ventured far from their sector for fear of a caning from Crone Maugriss. Dorian was no exception no matter how tough he put on.

Snatching the paper, Spud plodded off into the darkness.

"Where the hell're you going?" said Dorian.

"Gonna see what's in this sector. Didn't take you two for cowards."

Flushing, Dorian looked to Eli for support.

Eli shrugged. "If he's going, so am I."

Dorian snorted. "Fine, okay, we'll go, but don't expect me to haul your corpse back to Bolus if you spring some thief's trap, huh?"

It'd been five years since any of them had left their sector, when a leak that'd flooded the town of Bolus had forced them to camp in Ratskin Row. Eli remembered why he hated leaving. A mile below the Great City at its deepest and Hades knew how far across, the Guts were a nightmare-labyrinth of canals and corridors and secret rooms, all dank and dayless, wandered by thieves and bigrats and worse.

The boys crossed a metal bridge over a waste canal. No one knew how deep the waste flowed, not even the Crones. More drumfires lit a path along the rim of the canal. Stray newsprint papered the ground, stories bleared illegible and likely older than Dorian. They reached the passage labeled *4015*. A sludgefall gushed from it, all echoing thunder.

Dorian took his place at the head of the group, climbing the steel ladder into the passage. Spud slipped his poker in a pant-loop and followed. Eli climbed next, bare feet clanging on each rung, head heavy with doubts.

He didn't want to leave the sector. It was safe.

But his curiosity had gotten the better of him. If there were trees down here it would be the biggest find of their lives.

The three boys felt their way through the unlit passage, the concrete banks of the canal slick underfoot. Farther on, fresh drumfires broke the blackness. More passages led off from both banks, each labeled in the same faded blue block-print: *4024, 4025, 4026, 4027….*

When the boys reached *4060* they groaned; the passage wasn't on their side of the canal.

"Guess that's it," said Spud.

"Guess so." Eli sighed. "Better get back before Maug comes sniffing."

"You do that," said Dorian, stripping to his underclothes. "But don't expect me to share what I find."

Eli laughed. "What, you're gonna swim over?"

But Dorian probably could. His slim body was corded with muscle from a life of climbing and crawling.

Dorian tied his shoes and clothes into a ball and chucked them onto the far bank.

"We came this far," Dorian said, and dove into the canal with a heavy splash. He swam across the sewage, slapping and kicking like mad. The other boys cringed in disgust.

Dorian heaved himself onto the bank and shook off scum like a bigrat.

Eli laughed. "Nice going. Now the stream's filthy."

"Least he got a bath out of it," said Spud. "Bastard was starting to stink up the place."

Scowling, Dorian clawed handfuls of sludge off his face. "Your turn."

Spud shook his head. "No way."

"I'd fuck a sewer yowie before swimming through that," Eli said.

"With what?" Dorian said as he put on his clothes. "Your manhood's over here."

Eli's jaw tightened. He couldn't back down, not now, and Dorian knew it. Not after supporting Spud's decision to investigate the note. Without thinking, Eli jumped into the waste. He regretted it right away. A stench worse than all the world's corpses put together smothered him. He kept his mouth shut tight as he grappled with the current. All he could think about as he crossed the canal was murdering Dorian. When he felt cool concrete on his fingers he heaved himself onto the bank. The filth was in his nose and nails and armpits.

Dorian smirked, drilling sludge from his ears with a finger. "Should've removed your clothes first."

Eli forced down the urge to punch him. "This better be worth it."

"Your turn, Spud," shouted Dorian.

The weakest of the boys, Spud had a harder time against the current. He crawled out of the stream farther down the bank, then gathered up the fire poker and clothes he'd chucked across.

"You okay?" asked Eli.

Spud grunted.

Zone 4060 was pure darkness. The kind that made your head spin, that drop-kicked your balance. Eli took each step slowly, gingerly. He hadn't come this far to die in a thief's trap.

Click, spark, click. A small flame rose from Dorian's lighter. Dorian ignited one of the ripejohn's shoes with it.

"What're you doing?" said Spud.

"Improvising." Dorian skewered Spud's fire poker through the shoe.

Eli shook his head. "Could be weeks before we find another ripejohn to hoof."

"And we'll hoof him when we find him. Come on."

Now that they could see it this zone wasn't too different from their own. It had the same walkways and bridges and alcoves but no oil drums or newspapers. If anyone lived here they hadn't left a mark. Each alcove bore a number above it, like the passages. Eli eyed the walls for traps. Three years ago he'd tripped a wire and brought three drums studded with glass rolling out of a wall; a pink seam still ran down his shin from the slash one had given him. Not as fancy as Dorian's scars but enough to impress the girls in Bolus.

35…36…37, the alcoves read.

Eli's coat of sewage was stiffening. It made him sick. The burning shoe crackled softly. Something big and furry scurried away from them.

50…51…52….

Eli puzzled over the message. Trees needed light to grow, all the legends said that. Maybe the dead man had meant something else. Did thieves call umbrellas *trees* in their argot? But umbrellas weren't useful outside of leaky places. Maybe the trees were drawings on a wall. The Guts had a lot of art in strange places, chalk scrawls and blood murals, vibrant sneezes of graffiti.

The seventy-third alcove looked no different than the rest, save a narrow maintenance passage in its center.

Eli doubted there'd been maintenance down here for a long time. "Bet there's traps in there."

"If there was, the ripejohn we hoofed woulda sprung 'em going in," said Dorian.

"You first then," said Spud.

Dorian hesitated. Holding up the makeshift torch, he entered the narrow passage. Spud and Eli followed. Eli kept his hand on the walls, feeling they might close in at any moment. There was a word for the fear of tight places. He got gooseflesh thinking of all the stuff he'd seen in the Guts. A leg jammed in a pipe, white with blue veins like marble. Trying not to think about such things just made it harder not to.

"How deep does it go, Dorian?" said Eli.

The older boy coughed. "Deep. Christ it stinks."

"You sure that's not us?"

"Maybe it's some kinda gas," said Spud.

"Gas. But if it's flammable...." Eli cursed himself for not thinking of that before.

"Then we roast like rats on a spit," said Dorian. "Only if there was gas we'd be roasting already." He halted. "Look."

The left wall held a door, its window spidered with cracks.

"Maintenance room," said Dorian. He kicked open the door.

Inside, big bulky consoles lined the walls, their monitors dark and buttons buried in grey mold.

Nothing. They pressed on.

"Wonder how long it's been since anyone came through here," said Eli.

Dorian swiped a cobweb. "Since before we were born."

"How d'you know?"

"Crone Maugriss says whole crews used to come down here. They stopped when the thieves took over."

The walls came to an end.

"What's ahead?" asked Spud.

"It's--a *cave*." Dorian descended a rocky slope, allowing Eli to see past him. Their light caught the wet knuckled stone of the cave's far wall about fifty paces ahead. Stalactites fanged the ceiling; columns rose from lumps of flowstone to join them. A steel bridge spanned a trench, both ends bolted to rock.

Several pipes ran through the trench, red with rust.

Eli and Spud tried to keep up with Dorian but the uneven ground made hard work of their descent.

"Never seen a cave," said Eli. It was grander than he'd expected but eerie in its lack of symmetry. He was just happy to be out of the maintenance passage.

"This place'll lead us there, I can feel it," said Dorian.

Eli wasn't so sure. "Doesn't feel like part of the sewers. Might lead nowhere."

"Those pipes have to join another level of the Guts, or why would they be here? We didn't swim through all that shit to turn back now."

The boys crossed the bridge, then followed the pipes in the trench deeper into the cave.

Eli expected to hear bats and moles and bugs, but there was only the plink of dripstone, the soft flap of the fire. The air tasted like a thing long dead. Maybe a mass grave was nearby, a dumping ground for the serial killers said to roam the Guts. That would be something for the girls in Bolus to chew on. *Think you've seen some gross stuff? Wait till I tell you about the bodies we found.*

They crawled down a steep incline, losing skin on the way. The ground farther on was so bumpy they had to pause every now and then to knead the pain from their feet.

"What's that?" asked Dorian in a nervous hush.

They listened.

"Don't hear anything," said Spud.

"A low hiss." Dorian strained to listen. "Not far off."

"Like a gas leak?"

"No. Not like that."

A few paces ahead, the trench ended and the pipes disappeared into stone. Eli cursed. Just their luck.

Spud slumped against a mound of flowstone. "Now what?"

"We keep going till we find the trees," said Eli. "We can't quit now."

Dorian shook his head. "Without that stupid pipe, we're lost."

"After taking us through all that, you'd just turn around?"

"I'm brave, not stupid. But by all means keep going. I'll tell Maug you died a hero's death down here."

Eli snatched the torch from Dorian. "Good luck finding your way back. C'mon, Spud."

Dorian grabbed at the torch, but Eli was too quick for him.

"Give it here, Eli. I'll hurt you good."

Eli swished the torch out of Dorian's reach. Dorian seized Eli by the nape, pinching hard. Eli shouted. His foot caught a rock. He tripped, grabbing Dorian, and brought them both tumbling. Dorian smacked his head on the cave floor, hard.

The poker clattered to the ground; the burning shoe came loose and rolled.

Blood slicked Eli's hands and cheeks where the stone had skinned him. Pain bloomed in his neck. *The torch.* He groped in the dark for the fire poker. Where was it?

"Guys." Spud's voice, low and quavering.

"Hold on," said Eli.

"Guys."

Eli found the poker and speared the shoe. He raised the torch, cringing at the ache in his arm. Dorian was unconscious on the ground, a small patch of blood on his forehead.

"Help me, Spud." Eli tried to lift Dorian, but the boy was too heavy.

"There's…." Spud's voice trailed off.

"What?"

Then Eli saw it, a huge death-white snake brushing Spud's leg as it moved across the stone, hissing softly. To Eli's disgust and horror, the creature had no eyes. It crept over Dorian's calf then over the small of his back. It turned him with its body, enough to thread under him and back up then around him again, the coils tightening until snake and boy were one spool of flesh.

"Do something," Spud pleaded.

Fighting down panic, Eli did the first thing he could think of and nudged the torch into the snake's flank. White muscle twitched. The snake hissed louder.

Eli tried again and the coils around Dorian relaxed.

Spud stomped the snake's tail and the creature uncoiled completely, slithering off into the darkness.

"Watch Dorian," said Eli, and went after the snake.

It was wounded. It couldn't be far.

Spud called after him. Eli felt guilty for leaving them in the dark, but he had to kill the creature before it ambushed them again, had to crush that horrible eyeless head.

He chased a flicker of movement, ignoring his many aches. The ground gave way and he rolled down a slope, then got up and grabbed his torch, expecting the snake to strike. But he was alone.

A cave wall loomed ahead. In the wall was a concrete passage with faded blue letters: *Rest Station G.*

4060-73G. This was it.

"Where are you?" Spud's voice, echoing.

Eli waved the torch. "Down here! I've found it!"

"Kill it then."

"No, not that."

Spud appeared at the top of the slope, dragging Dorian. "Help."

Eli went to them and picked up Dorian's legs with one arm while holding the torch in the other. He and Spud maneuvered down the slope, then set down Dorian.

"Why'd you run off?" Spud demanded.

"Never mind. Look." Eli pointed to the passage.

Spud grinned for the first time in months.

Groaning, Dorian opened his eyes and touched the blood on his head.

"You alright?" said Eli.

"Jesus." Dorian regarded the blood with a dismal look. "What happened?"

Then he saw the passage and laughed. He stood, reaching for balance. "You have no idea where we are, do you?"

"I do," said Eli, then saw that no one bought it. "We can't be far."

"You're an idiot. But you've got more balls than I thought."

The passage opened to a smaller cave with an industrial-grey building set into the far wall. It had no windows, only a steel roll-up door with a black handle at the bottom. The boys took turns trying to lift the door, but it wouldn't budge.

Spud looked at the ripejohn's note. "'Trees. I seen them but the way in's too small.'"

"Not small to me," said Dorian.

"Maybe this isn't the way in."

A red streak on the ground caught Eli's eye. He stooped to smell. Blood. He tracked it to an empty trench leading out of the rest station, probably a defunct waste canal. A small grate in the trench led into the building. Eli held the torch to the iron mesh. He could just make out something tall and spindly in the station, but it might have been a trick of the light. He ripped off the grate, letting it drop with a clang.

Dorian and Spud crouched beside him.

"Too big for you and me, Eli," said Dorian. He looked at Spud.

Spud sighed. "I'll need the torch." Eli gave it to him, and he vanished through the hole.

Without any light, the cave's darkness was deeper than black.

Dorian rubbed his hands. "It's cold. Maug's worrying her herself crazy I bet."

Eli spat. "Think we'll make it back?"

"Not sure. No idea how I'll explain this wound, though."

"I'm still working on why we smell like shit."

Metal shrieked from the station entrance; the steel door rumbled open.

Spud emerged, awestruck. "You gotta see this."

Inside, their torch illuminated a world stranger and more beautiful than Eli could have imagined, like a place from some fable. A dead forest filled the building, branches bereft of leaves, bark ossified white and shot with cracks. The branches merged into one great net overhead. The trees were stone-still, but Eli could almost imagine them in the wilderness, the secrets they'd utter in the wind, the ancient things they knew.

Dead grass crunched as the boys explored the forest.

It was a crime to keep this place hidden. The people of Bolus would grow old and die knowing only the trees in old drawings or in the bedtime stories of Crones. The dead trees of the rest station held more life than Bolus, than the Guts, than anywhere.

"Something up there!" shouted Spud.

Eli raised the torch. Sure enough the eyeless snake was sheltering high in the boughs, slack hanging in pale parabolas. Blood dripped from its tail, staining white bark.

Spud swallowed. "It tried to eat you, Dorian. Kill it while you can."

Eli wanted to agree. But the snake's helplessness moved him. They weren't much better than the snake, after all, just desperate creatures of the darkness like it. "Leave it. It's dying anyway."

"No. *Kill it*," said Spud.

Dorian grabbed the torch from Eli and moved to strike.

Eli grabbed Dorian's arm. "The snake didn't bring us down here. We came ourselves. Leave it."

Dorian glared, but to Eli's surprise he didn't argue. He just frowned and lowered the torch.

"You coulda just told me it's your kin," he snarked.

An hour of scouring the rest station turned up ancient documents and corroded work tools and food black with age. But no shoes or gum sticks or cigarettes. Nothing they could trade in Bolus, at least not until Eli dredged a bulky flashlight out of a busted storage locker. He rubbed the dust off its pane, then flicked the switch a few times and shook the thing until its light punched the dark, a dim yellow. He grinned. It was something, at least.

They stuffed their loot into a wrinkly black duffel bag they found, and Dorian slung this over his shoulder. As they clambered back up the slope outside the rest station, talking about what the girls in Bolus would think of them and how hard a caning they'd get, Spud paused with a look of revelation.

"What's the matter?" said Eli.

Spud shook his head. "Just hit me. We might be the last people in the world to ever see them."

"See what?"

"Trees," said Spud.

Eli glanced back at the rest station entrance, feeling a chill on the air, listening. If the trees had any last secrets he wanted to hear them. But there was only silence, as cold and unyielding as the stone.

———✦———

Jordan Chase-Young is an American-Australian SFF writer. His stories have recently appeared in Metaphorosis, Unidentified Funny Objects 8, and the Zombies Need Brains anthology When Worlds Collide, among other venues. He writes about the future at ebookofthenewsun.wordpress.com and tweets under @jachaseyoung.

Skin Deep

Celine Low

It was the ink, I was sure of it. No matter how carefully I stencilled my designs, they always turned out strange. Once my needles pierced the skin, the colours seemed to *sink*—not just into flesh, but into reality itself.

This sleeve I was finishing for Mod, for example. My stomach was a tangled knot of nerves, because Mod Balig was the new leader of the Werewerms, the largest gang in Bel Loréth next to the Crazy Crows. The Werewerms were small but they were growing fast, fattening their purses from the monthly fees they squeezed from the shops within their turf. Mod didn't get to where he was without breaking a few heads, and if I wasn't careful mine would be one of them.

I straightened, stretching my spine. Mod's bedroom wasn't the most conducive place for inking—the chair was uncomfortably hard—but he'd refused to come to Skin Deep. I had to bring all my stuff to his, just so he could have a girl massage his feet at the same time. The girl knelt beside me now, slender hands kneading his calves. Her scent wafted over: wood and amber, slightly floral. Masculine, with a trace of feminine.

I told myself to focus, angling my head to examine my work. Something felt off about it, like everything I'd inked since I'd opened Skin Deep. Usually everyone had an aura, the vibes emanating from mood, personal history and the cloud of possibilities shimmering around an individual. I did my designs based on my perception of this aura, and if I was right, the customer would like my ideas. But recently, I'd been feeling that

10

as I worked, the weave of reality around a person was being *re-stitched*. So much so that I was questioning my sanity. Because by the time I was done with each piece I could no longer sense the initial aura—only the inked image, crystallised in flesh.

Mod had asked for a dragon. A classic, nothing special, but Mod wanted a new marking for the Werms to show a change of leadership. So I'd carved a dragon round his arm, obsidian wings unfolding like thunderclouds eclipsing the sun. At the edges of my vision the dragon's scales rippled, deepwater-black and green. The air felt heavy, bloated with strange magic.

Mod fidgeted. The dragon moved with his muscles, rising and coiling, ready to strike. "Hold still," I snapped. My hand wobbled. A drop of ink fell on his pants.

"Watch it, boy!" Mod snarled.

Mod looked near to losing his temper, but thankfully the door burst open and a little girl scampered in, followed by a harried-looking woman.

"Papa! Papa!" the girl cried. "Risha slapped me."

"It was just—I didn't hit hard, I swear—she refused to—"

Mod shot to his feet, his face reddening. "How *dare* you hit my daughter?" His palm shot out; the girl's caretaker shrieked as it connected with her cheek. "Do I pay you to hit my children, huh?"

I flinched with every echoing slap.

Beside me, Mod's masseuse dried her hands on a towel. "He has a temper," she whispered to me. "It will pass."

The little girl, who had been watching with an impish smirk, now bit her lip. "Papa," she said, hugging his leg, "Papa, she didn't mean it, she didn't hit me so hard, and I was naughty."

It was like watching the end of a storm. Mod softened, picking the girl up and kissing her forehead.

"Still," he growled, glaring at the sobbing babysitter. "You're fired."

He settled his daughter on his lap, and barked at me. "Well?"

I jumped, muttered an apology the-gods-know-what, and dipped my needles again into the yellow.

The crusty yellow of blistered skin. The poison-yellow of wild parsnip. The cruel yellow of a desert sun.

Mod's masseuse leaned in to peer at my finishing strokes, her grey eyes widening in fascination. "So life-like," she murmured. Her skin was a velvety taupe-brown, silver under the light. "It's as if … it's tearing out of his skin."

Amber for the dragon's iris, like glowing coal. Cadmium flaring over veins of burnt umber. These were the shades I saw in Mod, a consolidation of his volcanic anger, his patient greed, his rough-hewn hunger. There'd been more to him when he'd walked in, I was sure, but now I couldn't see him being anything else.

Beneath my hand, black pupils narrowed into slits.

The inks had been left behind by Shu, the lady who'd sold me my shophouse. After spending all my coin on drink and inns, I'd paid her with the only valuable thing I'd had left—the gold stylus my parents had given me for my fifteenth birthday, two years ago.

Good riddance. It was a fine blade with an ornate handle meant for runewriting, but the complicated grammar and logographs of runes had never given me anything but headaches.

My mother was the Imperial Healer and headmistress of the Amari Academy of Bel Loréth, and she had never let me forget that I was Amari, too.

More precisely, that I was born to be a terraformer, like her. Amari have natural predilections towards different states of matter, and terraformers supposedly share the very essence of Earth—solids—just as tideraisers partake of the liquid character of Water, and windriders of Air, the gaseous element of steam and fire.

On nights when I particularly missed home, I'd dream of my mother. She had loved me, once. I dreamed of the gardens in our manor, the air thick with jasmine. My mother's hair glowing wheat-gold, twining itself into twigs and vines. Her hands reaching for me, the veins in her arms twisting into green tendrils. And her voice, ancient as pine. *This is your heritage—the shaping of stone, metal, soil, flesh. A skilled terraformer understands the workings of the body, and heals by moulding the dust from which man is made. Learn, and continue our legacy.*

She lifted a hand and a rowan sapling sprung from the ground, unfurling into a tree. *Vision and gesture,* she said, *the principles on which Amari power is founded. Ours is a weak remnant of the divine creative force, a leftover from the time gods roamed the earth. Have you learned the runes I showed you?*

I shuffled my feet. *But Amari don't need runes,* I whined.

Vision and gesture might command matter in the moment, but runes, like written contracts, keep a spell binding even in their author's absence. Otherwise, matter reverts to its natural laws.

She took out a stylus from the folds of her robes, the blade so sharp I only hissed in pain a moment later. Blood welled on my palm, forming intricate lines arranged in neat word-squares. *For protection,* she said, *against scrapes and bruises.* The rune shimmered, sinking beneath my skin. She moved her hand over mine and the cuts faded, but for a long time I felt it there, the weighty sting of her love.

That afternoon after I left Mod's house, his masseuse came to Skin Deep.

"What will you give me?" she asked, smiling at me with her eyes—teardrop-shaped and grey-green, like rainclouds scudding a forest lake.

I considered her swan limbs, the softness of her gaze, the hardness of her jaw.

"Wisteria," I said. She flinched.

I frowned. I usually got it right the first time.

Her aura flickered around her. I sensed a certain fragility, but a doggedness, too. "A candle-flame?" I hazarded. "A symbol of evanescence and the everyday fight for light in darkness."

She tilted her head, considering. "And of vulnerability, the flame naked without its paper-lantern dress." Then a rakish grin flashed over her face like armour and she leaned over the counter, her movements languid, feline. "Wouldn't you like to see me naked," she drawled. Her eyes gleamed, suddenly more green than grey.

"Um. What about the Trickster? Pékuras the shapeshifter, who escaped hell in the form of a cat."

In Lorétheian myth, cats could travel between the mortal and spirit realms. I pointed to a small sketch I'd done of a boy turning into a black cat, leaping into a white light while ghostly hands reached for him from beneath. "Patron of merchants and travellers," I added, in case she was one.

"A trickster?" She arched an eyebrow. "I assure you I'm honest."

"I didn't mean—"

She smirked, enjoying my embarrassment.

"Why wisteria?" she asked.

"Ištara's flower. Bliss, tenderness, immortality." I imagined a wash of purple against the cool undertones of her skin.

"The Loréthian goddess of love."

I nodded, shrugged. "I don't know the Bharan gods, but if you have an image I could copy …"

"I already have them."

She raised a sleeve to reveal smooth skin. I stared, puzzled. Then she slid a hand over her right forearm and colour bled in, beryl-bright blue-green feathers with iridescent eyes. "The Creator," she said. She lifted her other arm, where stark black lines crossed to form twin spears. "And the Destroyer. God of death, war, retribution."

"You're a terraformer," I breathed. That wasn't why I was amazed; I knew that terraformers' flesh-altering abilities made them excellent at disguise, though they couldn't completely shapeshift. Neither was it the intricacy of detail that astounded me, nor the impossible vividness of hue. What caught my breath was the *weight* of each image, as if reality bent around it, answered its call.

"A Namer, like you," she said. "You glimpse a fragment of a person's soul and you draw it out. The ink seeps into flesh, mingles with blood. The body transforms, and the mind with it."

"This is … a kind of Earth magic?"

She nodded. "But this power isn't just something you're born with. It's also the medium—some inks, like Shu's, help you *see* things better when you're working."

I stared down at my hands.

"Your use of power doesn't make you less of an artist," she said gently. "Your design must be true, an image that binds to body and mind. Runes act the same way, like chains you can pull to command matter, and through matter, reality itself—just as the form and habits of the body sculpt the mind. And, like any art, truth can only be conveyed through technique."

With what little terraforming skill I had, I'd shaped a needle-brush that could vibrate the pins more quickly than human hands could move. This allowed me use horizontal strokes for subtle shading and soft gradients—a technique I was proud of. The girl's peacock feathers, however, were rendered with such precision that skin morphed into brilliant plumage, and as my eyes moved over her arm, each wispy strand billowed hypnotizingly as if touched by an imaginary breeze.

She dropped her sleeve, suddenly self-conscious. "I've never been able to do it for others. Only on myself. And there are parts of me that I can't reach."

How could I resist? She came every few days, disrobing before me while the summer sun warmed us through the window.

"How did a rich boy like you end up here?" she asked, once the awkwardness between us had passed. "You talk like you're from Jewel."

Bel Loréth was a city made up of two lake-islands, known colloquially as Jewel and the Claw. Each faced the other like its mirror image. But while the Temple was Jewel's crowning glory, Hogshead, the pleasure district, was the Claw's. Shortly after my fifteenth birthday, I'd hopped on a barge to Hogshead and never looked back.

"Why else would a rich boy cross over? To join the degenerates at Hogshead, of course."

She cast me a cool glance. "Did you like tossing coin at the women?"

I paused, startled. "I was usually too drunk for women."

Her shoulders remained stiff. I cringed at the impression I was giving, but I held her gaze.

"I hate it," she muttered. The vehemence in her voice surprised me. "This whole filthy city."

"Burn it down, then," I said mildly. "What's stopping you?"

She blinked, then laughed. "The sunstone and stained glass won't burn—didn't you learn this in school? The buildings won't get so much as a scratch. You need to make better jokes, boy."

"I make first-rate jokes, girl."

She smiled. "So how'd you end up here, all sweet and sober?"

"I was walking off a hangover. Saw an old man at Craft Lane, his client wearing a full suit. The old man's art brought that body to life."

How could I describe how my eyes had burned, the strange elation I'd felt at the sight of those colours soaking the skin, the promise of what I could do to guide a soul into its identity?

I could not. But from the way she was looking at me, I had a feeling she understood.

So I said simply, "I volunteered to be his assistant."

She nodded, turning back to face the window.

Her eyes drifted far away, reflecting the cerulean lake beyond. "Do you miss home?"

I thought of Jewel's stately mansions and sparkling canals, where I'd spent my happy childhood. My mother's disappointment had only shown as I'd grown older. She became sarcastic and bitter. She made herself take cruel measures.

We had a maid whose six-year-old son we took in after the maid died. After I'd failed my healer examinations, my mother brought him before me. He lay drugged on the carpet, blood seeping from a slit in his wrist. "Heal him," my mother commanded. She stood watching, arms folded, anchoring me to the chair with her roots and vines.

It wasn't a deep gash. Any terraformer could've done it in a heartbeat, just by sight. I sobbed. The pool of red spread across the floor.

I couldn't look at the boy, so I kept my gaze on the window, at the hill on which the Temple of the Thousand Gods glittered, stabbing the sky with its salt-white sunstone towers, its dazzling stained-glass spires. I remembered the stories told about these structures, how all this glass was blown by the Amari of old. My forefathers. I looked down at my hands.

I groped for my magic, until my eyes teared and my fingers ached. I wrestled against my mother's chains. I thought of the wisteria in the Temple courtyard, a tree old as the hills, its vast canopy dripping with the same purple vines constricting my legs. *Bliss, tenderness, immortality.* I prayed.

In the morning my mother knelt before the boy, crimson staining her robes. She closed her eyes, head bowed. Then she scooped him up gently, and left without a word.

I hadn't even known his name.

Mod's girl gazed steadily at me, her eyes flint-grey, piercing.

I gave a little laugh. "Other than the hot baths and rose-scented towels? No, I don't miss home."

She raised her brows.

"My parents aren't very nice people," I told her.

She sighed. "Who is?"

My thoughts dwelled, more and more, on Mod's girl. She was indentured, she said. She showed me the mark of the dragon on her wrist. She wasn't just a masseuse; she did other work for him, too. But what work, she refused to say, and I didn't want to know.

I wrote on the curves of her back and the canvas of her soul, each letter a pinprick of colour and pain. I gave her a whole tree, roots sinking into hip, jet branches arching up her spine, the crown a watercolour-spray of purple.

"After all this time," I said to her, "I still don't know your name."

She smiled and told me I did. So I called her Wisteria, Wisteria of the Moonlit Garden, Wisteria of ancient longing and transient trysts.

We never met outside of Skin Deep, though sometimes after a session we'd walk along the lake. She said I made her feel uncomfortable, because I saw into her soul. But perhaps it's a pleasurable thing, to be so pierced by another. Because she kept coming, even when the needle-wounds of our previous session had not yet healed. She brought all of her enigmatic love to me, allowing me to pore over her body with my eyes, my ink, my hands. She was a text I could not fathom, different with each read. So unlike me, yet she became a part of me. And when I made her cry my name out in bliss, she said this itself was a form of magic.

It was the oldest power in the world, and she showed me how to cast this spell, with vision, gesture and word, just as she cast it on me.

I rushed out when the first screams started.

In the sky was a monster of my creation, a figment of myth made real. I stood stupefied as the beast with obsidian wings swooped low and snarled, its massive bulk blocking the sun. I glimpsed rows of serrated teeth as from its gaping maw gushed rivers of red.

Shrieks descended into sobs of horror. Smoke welled, dimming the horizon. Flames licked the rooftops beyond the nearest shophouses.

I bolted back in and locked myself upstairs. Wisteria—I should've asked her where she lived. I was pacing by the bed when a glimmer beyond the window froze my heart again.

Behind the trees, the lake rose.

A tideraiser rode the crest of the wave, her body foaming, misting up in spray. Above her the amorphous shape of a windrider flew with his arms outstretched, pushing the tide forward with a squall that shook the trees by the shore. Intermittently the windrider would vaporise into a cloud that pulsed and dissipated and coalesced again into the faint semblance of a man, his storm-grey bowels sparking with lightning as he gathered mass and force. The effect was surreal and jarring, a bruise punched into the middle of a sunlit lake above a frothing wall of teal.

I slammed my windows shut.

The lake crashed down. It spurted up against the rocks and surged through the trees. It struck the walls like thunder. Windows rattled. I fell beside my bed as the floor spasmed.

Then there was only the loud sloosh of water as it gushed through the Claw. Wails rang through the thin walls, and muffled lapping from downstairs told me that the lake was spilling in.

When a smidgen of calm returned, I waded through the mucky water and debris, leaving the door open to let the water drain. It was only knee-deep, thank the gods, but I'd have to throw out most of my furniture.

I thought, vaguely, to search for her. I didn't even have her name, not any that would be recognised. Still, I wandered through the flood, hoping.

All noise whittled down to silence when I turned into Fortune Street, where Mod's house was.

Since the Claw was a gaudy replica of Jewel, all the sunstone and stained-glass buildings held up, but the poor suffered most, as usual. Squatter dwellings sat in sad, soggy ruins. Luckily the gangs had to curb their own penchant for violence; damaged shops meant less to extort.

A shadow passed overhead. The dragon dived down.

Its bulk diminished, wings folding into arms as it metamorphosised into Mod. He rushed into the burned remains of a building with a bellow of such grief that I felt a squeeze of panic—was Wisteria in there, bones crumbling to ash? I stumbled forward, my flapping wet trousers slowing me down.

Mod spotted me as I was scrabbling through the charred heap. "My daughter," he said blankly, almost like a question.

I didn't know what to say. Hesitantly, I reached out to lay a hand on his shoulder. He continued speaking in that same hollow voice, as if he was trying to make sense of the mess he'd made.

"I meant to target Flint Street. Just the Crows' houses. But once I started …" He shuddered. "I couldn't stop. I wanted to see it all burn. The anger felt good."

His wrath was sudden and terrible. He shoved my hand away and whirled on me, his face contorted. "*You* did this," he snarled, grabbing my collar and lifting me clean off the ground. "You turned me into this—this *monster*." His huge fist shook, and my body shook with it. "*You killed my daughter*," he roared, and a world of anguish flamed into fury as the dragon slithered up his neck.

Something slammed into him from behind. I collapsed with a splash, choking with terror and relief.

The Crows were the oldest, biggest gang in the Claw, and they would not go down easy. They came for him now, their tideraiser from one end of the street and their windrider from another, the two Amari raising their hands to attack. Their bodies dispersed sporadically into spray and vapour, but as their sleeves fell back I glimpsed the Crows' mark on their left wrists.

The windrider's palm struck the air like a slap. A gale shrieked through the street. The tideraiser made another gesture and the flood began to boil.

Mod leapt into the air, great wings unfurling. Fire erupted from his mouth. I flinched, the sudden wave of heat scorching.

No time to run.

But the windrider flicked his wrists, and the flames hit an invisible shield and sputtered out, devoid of oxygen.

The dragon fled. The windrider vaporised, shooting after him. A shadow over the sun—they were gone.

A garish sunset washed over the empty street, turning the water to blood. I wondered how many had survived. The tideraiser must have been thinking along the same lines, because she sighed and lifted her arms again. I shied away, but as water trickled from the surviving houses, I realised she was sweeping out the flood.

"Go home," she snapped, when she caught me staring.

I plodded through the streets until dawn broke the next day and I returned, drenched and muddy, to Skin Deep. I thought I'd never be able to fall asleep but I must have, because I heard Wisteria calling. Her face multiplied before me, dissolving in mist. I saw the tree still half-complete on her back, a blur of scattered petals, colours fading.

For months, I waited. I repaired what I could of Skin Deep, threw out what I couldn't. I thought, then tried not to think, of the monster I'd made. The people Mod had killed. Did he have a choice, or did I rob him of it?

Did it matter? They were still dead.

When Wisteria finally came again, I hid my face so she wouldn't see how I almost wept when I saw her. My tongue felt swollen, blocking my throat, so I turned her around and poured myself into filling in her back.

"It's been chaos," she said. "Mod's pals are dead; the Werms have been fighting among themselves. Now the new boss has called a truce with the Crows. Mod's just biding his time, though—I know him. He'll keep coming until the Crows are destroyed. He'll keep coming for you. Zy, you have to leave."

I focused on the contour of her shoulders, using them to suggest a hint of mist.

She turned to stare at me.

"It's not your fault, Zy. You couldn't have known. The anger was in him all along, and it's far easier to blame others for our own flaws."

I shook my head. "I reduced him," I rasped, "to a flat image. A one-dimensional idea. I took away his capacity for change."

Thoughtfully, she studied her arm, letting ripples of blue-green play beneath her fingertips. "No image is one-dimensional. No one is incapable of change."

I etched in the last few branches.

"With Mod gone," I said, "does this mean you're free?"

"I still serve the Werms—or whoever commands them."

I'd tried to work slowly, but the end was inevitable. Shu's ink was running out. I only had black left, and it was down to the dregs.

"Why do you hide them?" I asked later, as we lay tangled in each other's limbs on my bed upstairs. I traced the soft contour of her arm, the peacock plumes hidden beneath her silver-birch skin.

She glanced away. "To survive," she said flatly. Then she looked at me and decided to trust. "I belonged to the Thousand-Flower Court. I couldn't let people see … who I was."

"And now?"

"Mod bought my contract a year ago. He needed someone charming but forgettable. I get close to powerful people and make them talk. Sometimes I threaten, sometimes I kill. So I'm faceless, nameless"—she rolled over, pecked me on the lips—"except with you."

I didn't ask how many she'd killed.

Another troubling thought struck me. "You should've told me. I wouldn't have—" I gestured at her back, the punctures I'd made. Wounds not yet healed.

"No, I wanted the truth you saw."

"Was there any … Wisteria?"

Her smile grew sad. "Many. There was Jasmine, Sakura, Orchid … Only the wealthiest can afford a Wisteria. It's Ištara's flower, after all." She put a hand over mine. "But they were never like me. This"—she gestured at her back—"is your Wisteria."

I laced my fingers in hers. Her hand was calloused, used to hard work, unlike mine. "Flee with me. Or … the Crown could use you—"

"I have had enough of being used. Besides …" She sat up and touched her foot. A rune appeared, blood-red and pulsing, knife-cuts etched into her right sole. She sighed. "It keeps me within the Claw. Two years, Mod promised. Then I am free."

"You trust him? He's ruled by anger."

"My contract with the Crows was ninety-nine years. I was twelve when they kidnapped me. They didn't want to break my skin, so they kicked my legs open and filled me with crushed firefruit. Again and again until I performed. Mod offered me hope."

That glint in her eyes.

"And vengeance," I murmured.

She was quiet.

"Thank you," she said softly, "for your gift. It's made me a little more whole. I could never have touched you without it, could never have loved. And now I've found a way to use it—as a weapon." She raised her chin. "Tonight, I return to the Thousand-Flower Court."

"As a spy," I spat, "dressed as the goddess of love."

Her gaze on me was steel. "They'll see me and love me. Then I'll kill the man who took my innocence."

Nothing left but pitch-black stains on the tips of my needles. Nothing I could do to save the woman I loved.

I pressed my black-tipped needles into my skin, on the inside of my wrist. I wanted to give myself twin spears, but all I succeeded in making was a meaningless smudge, like the shadow of a falling leaf.

That night, silently, I followed her.

I slipped through the throng—the gamblers and revellers of Hogshead, the silk-robed gentry in their palanquins, into the vine-wreathed arcades and stained-glass atria of the Thousand-Flower Court.

No one noticed; my name was Shadow.

Invisible, bodiless, I lurked in a corner as she danced, lilac silks streaming around her willow frame. On her exposed back was the tree I'd carved, petals eddying as she twirled. I saw eyes bright with desire, men's and women's both, knees weak before this shining Ištara. When she was done a profound hush fell over the hall, as though her dance had been sacred. Then the whispers:

Beautiful

ah, unrivalled

How much do you think—

Wisteria, wisteria, her Name susurrated through the hall, rising to a crescendo as the audience shouted their bids. But the Court was owned by Raf Gola, king of the Crows, and if Raf wanted a Flower, no one opposed him.

And how could he not want her? That night, everyone was touched by her light. Perhaps they felt, as I did when I watched her, that the lines between all souls softened, and in that catch of breath we could break free of ourselves. Even Raf, I think, fell a little in love with her.

Already he had marked her: three crows on the left wrist. With Mod gone, the rune that bound her in the Claw for two years, a contract binding in flesh, could now be owned by him. How much had Raf paid the Werms for it?

He took her by the elbow, two henchmen trailing behind. We meandered up a spiralling staircase and into a cavernous chamber, high-ceilinged, marble-floored, walls of stained glass backlit by the balcony's lanterns.

Raf left his men guarding the door. I skulked in the darkness as she pulled him to her.

They lit no candles. The windows threw light around like a prism, the bed a luminous altar. He lay her down, and her body moulded itself to his like mercury. And as he buried his face in her neck, she reached up, slowly, to pull a slender blade from the voluminous whorls of her hair.

It was my fault. I had bound her with a name inscribed on flesh. For as the dragon could not control his rage, so Wisteria, Ištara, goddess of love, could not kill.

Their bodies rose and fell together, rose and fell, and the knife hovered behind his back, catching colour like a butterfly wing.

Then Raf sat up to turn her over, and grim realisation darkened his features while beneath him Wisteria still reached for him, lips parted, cheeks flushed. Was she struggling, as Love clashed with Vengeance? Did those twin spears flicker on her arm, before his cloak cast a pall over her?

The shadows fell uselessly around them.

I could only watch as he pried the knife from her fingers, and tenderly, regretfully— as if it were a waste to kill such beauty— plunged it into her heart.

When the door clicked shut I materialised, cradling her in my arms; too stunned to weep, too scared to scream. Her eyes were closed, her mouth still open as if in bliss.

A terraformer could've saved her.

But I was a Namer with no ink, a gangly boy with too-soft skin, barely a man. What could I do against the king of the Crows?

What could I do, as Shadow? I followed him.

I took his sight so that he staggered, wild-eyed and raving as he crashed down the stairs. His men shouted in confusion and hurried to support him, and I blinded them, too. I thought that was all I could do. I had Named myself. I was only shadow.

But I was pure grief, mad with it, and I found more.

Shadow lengthened, gained form and texture, became a cloud. The men ran in panic as the cloud grew, filling the halls, suffocating.

It was still just smoke, immaterial.

Then Cloud became Shroud, and Shroud wrapped itself tight around Raf's body, revelling in his muffled screams. It dragged him through the air and over the city, binding his face like a second skin. And when it reached the mirror-dark lake, it shoved him in.

His throat opened. Water gushed in. I felt his body buck.

As his dark robes sank beneath me, I rose, swelling gently with the last bubbles of his breath. And I mourned, for it was not only Wisteria I had lost.

Summer again, a sultry moon. A black cat darts past my window.

The door swings open and a boy enters Skin Deep, his features vaguely familiar, his slanting eyes impossibly green. He walks straight up to me as if he knows me and hands me a jar of tarry ink. "Another one for the road?" he says.

I frown.

"Shu's ink." A smirk flirts about his lips, and I begin to like him, despite my bemusement. "I found her and persuaded her to give me the formula."

The boy grows serious. "Raf's dead; the rune no longer holds me. We can leave the Claw together, go somewhere Mod won't find us." He looks around, lips quirking up again. "You need new furniture, anyway."

Lips I have kissed.

She stands before me with a naughty gleam, a strange boy with scruffy hair but whose aura I recognise nonetheless. "How—" I am lost for words.

She spreads her arms and shows me. Her skin bursts to life in a riot of colour, diaphanous panes shifting and overlapping; picture after picture layered one on another, saturating every spot her hands can reach. The Creator with his blue-green plumes, the Destroyer with his spears. There were Lorétheian gods too: a cat with dangerous eyes, typifying the Trickster whose boyish form she'd taken; a tree bowed like an offering, its crown laden with wisteria. And more, not just gods but symbols, all runes in their own right.

For a long time, I stare. Then I understand. After all, isn't that what a god is—a rune, a word-image of transformative power? As Trickster, she evaded hell. As Warrior, she wrestled back to life. As Creator, she would forge a new beginning, and as Love, she would do it with me.

"I have many names," they say, laughing, "many faces, many lives. We are what we make ourselves—so we picked our selves up, and climbed out of hell."

They say this like it's the easiest thing in the world.

"What about vengeance?" I ask. "I robbed it from you."

Wisteria smiles, their eyes the calm of evening. "There will be justice. But if all men are equal, then no one alone can be its arbiter. Vengeance was never mine to take."

I frown, incredulous. "If I hadn't killed him, you would have let him go?"

"Ah, so it was you."

I swallow. Wisteria tilts their head, searching for the words.

"For so long," they murmur, "we carried vengeance in our heart. It was a crushing weight, consuming, corrosive. It did not let me live."

"You would forget all he's done to you? What about all he would have done to others?"

Wisteria spreads their hands. "There is law."

I shake my head. "The laws are decided by the powerful."

"Should I then claim power for myself?"

I bite my lip.

They try again. They come close to take my hand, placing a palm over my chest. "Listen."

My heart leaps to meet their fingers.

"When Love looked into the eyes of her neighbour," Wisteria whispers, their gaze on me clear and penetrating, "she saw his soul—and it was indistinguishable from hers. She saw the violence of his parents and his grandparents and further back still, experienced the whole web of actions and consequences that shaped him finally into the monster that killed her, again and again, within himself. In a single breath, Love lived his life, and he could be her enemy no longer."

On their skin a wash of purple; in their eyes a glimmer of tears. Then they grow strong and hard and the twin spears flash like lightning in their hands, even as wisterias cascade across the ground. "Yet Love was also every soul he had destroyed, and we were still the girl whose life he'd stolen. Justice must be done—but we didn't want it done that way. So we destroyed the hate within ourselves. And then …" They turn away to face the window, moonlight silvering their cheeks. "We went to hell."

I watch, entranced, as petals spill over my feet.

"We felt our body return like a cloak over our soul, gathering itself from the ash it had become. We could be anything we wanted. We were a cat. We were a boy. We were a woman. We were more."

"But Raf …" I cannot let it go. I have to justify myself. "You understand, don't you? He had to be punished."

Wisteria lowers their head. "I understand."

When they speak again, their voice is soft with sorrow, and their words sound slow and distant, like a priestly parable, or a storyteller's tale of far-off lands.

"We saw him, on our way out. The king of the Crows on hell's barren plains, digging himself into a pit. He could have walked out any time he wanted, but he kept digging. Perhaps he'll dig forever. Or perhaps he'll find his way through the hell of his own making, someday understanding enough to turn around." Wisteria sighs, a breath like many winds. "Who, after all, is innocent? We are none of us alone. We'll all pay, in some way, for the blood on our hands."

I think of the body of the man I killed, rotting in the deep. A baby burning in the ruins, a man possessed by rage. A boy whose name I should have known.

Wisteria turns back to me. Their eyes are bright and sharp again, irises the jewel-green of spring. "Yet," they say, and the echo of their voices fill the room, fill my heart, as a myriad faces veil one another, and grin. "Yet through it all, we'll live."

I gather them all in Shadow, and leap into the night.

Celine Low is a writer, painter, dancer and educator in Singapore and India. Her poetry, fiction and art have appeared in Sky Island Journal, Beyond Words, The Temz Review and Balloons Literary Journal, among other literary magazines. She has written articles for Book Riot and has ghostwritten thrillers, enrichment curricula and recipe books for fairies. Celine holds an MA in English Literature from the National University of Singapore where she did her dissertations on Tolkien and on the intersection of contemporary literature and architecture

Cara Cognatio

Nancy Pica Renken

How many ways can a jar of spaghetti sauce kill you? Sure, pasta sauce if you prefer. But for me, it was definitely spaghetti sauce that had it in for me because I've always hated spaghetti. Spaghetti is a mess. Those noodles? Way too long and sloppy. Do they ever stay rolled up nice on your fork? See? I don't care if you get fancy and use a spoon to roll up those damn noodles. They still unwind. Regardless, as strange as it may sound, those jars in my tiny pantry, next to boxes of real noodles like penne, ziti or mostaccioli, had a death wish for me.

My name is Tony and I'm a second-generation, Italian American. I'm named for St. Anthony, patron saint of Sorrento, the town in southern Italy my grandfather had to leave behind as a boy when his family immigrated to the States. My father is also named Tony, and my grandfather—you've guessed it. Apparently, every self-respecting Italian family has at least one Tony, regardless of patron saint, and many families have multiples. Growing up, I was *Little*

Tony, which I hated. My father was *Junior*. And, I never had the chance to meet my grandfather. He died before I was born, but I've been told that he had a passion for homemade spaghetti and celebrating family. Apparently, every Sunday evening his family would gather with their eleven children and have a pasta feast. And when the children married, they were expected to bring their spouses and kids for these impressive, crowded, loud feasts. I can only imagine as I wasn't there.

When my grandfather died, my father, feverishly devoted to making the ancestral recipe, carried on the tradition of Sunday gatherings. I remember studying at the kitchen table as a boy and inhaling that sweet aroma of basil, oregano, garlic-- simmering in the slow-cooked tomato sauce as he shaped meatballs out of ground pork and beef. My stomach growled as I scribbled answers. (*"Hey Dad, can we do a different noodle this time? Maybe penne? Short fat noodles are easier to spear." "No! Must be spaghetti!"*) I thought that sauce wafted straight to heaven, making both Tonys smile—my grandfather and the good saint, but now, I'm not so sure.

You see, dad came to visit me two weeks ago and rummaged through the pantry for the "real coffee in a can" that I keep just for him because he won't use my Keurig. He's informed me that, "real coffee doesn't come in little plastic cups and I don't want to drink plastic coffee, thank you very much." So, I buy him his favorite, generic, decaf coffee and drink it with him. It makes him happy and had become our tradition. But that day, I had just shopped on my limited, teacher budget and stocked up on penne and ten jars of that damn spaghetti sauce.

"Oh, Little Tony, what have you done?"

First, I cringe when he calls me that. Second, what had I done? I had always been studious. Straight laced. Boring. What could he have found? Not like I had a stash of pot or moonshine in there.

There were genuine tears in his eyes.

"How—How can you eat this stuff? Real spaghetti sauce doesn't come in a jar! Son, I'm so disappointed. What would your grandfather think?"

"Dad, I don't have the time to simmer the sauce or make *non-spaghetti* noodles by hand. I live alone. I teach all day. Besides, cooking was your thing, not mine."

His sad puppy eyes bored into mine. Silently, he held up the can of decaf and I made slow-drip coffee for him. He sat in my cramped, utilitarian, apartment kitchen, slumped in my extra chair, sipping his decaf and muttering yeses and no's through tight lips as if someone had kicked his favorite dog. He barely looked at me when he left that afternoon. All because I had committed the mortal sin of buying jarred spaghetti sauce.

I shut the door, shrugged, and settled down at the table (having just brewed some *real* coffee) to grade unimaginative, sophomore history essays.

Crash!

My head jerked up with a thin line of drool connected to the essay recently serving as my pillow.

"What the hell?"

A jar of spaghetti sauce lay shattered on the tile next to me, almost as if it had perched precariously on the ledge above me. But, I hadn't put a jar of sauce on the shelf. I wiped the drool off my chin and picked large shards out of the mess. *Dad must have placed it there. Yeah.* I cleaned up the mess and returned to grading.

The next morning, I awoke staring up into blurred, reddish glass. Moving to grab my glasses, a jar of sauce thumped onto my pillow where mere moments before, my head had lain. I stared at the insidious jar of spaghetti sauce. I knew I hadn't placed it on the shelf above my bed. I grabbed the murderous jar and set it down next to the Keurig on the kitchen counter. I brewed my bold blend and lifted the oversized mug to my lips. I stared at the jar. It stared back. I sighed as I glanced at the clock. I showered quickly, dressed, and got my butt to school.

The rest of my day was thankfully uneventful. The vindictive jar of sauce was still by the Keurig. I grabbed it and stashed it back in the pantry. I cooked a burger and settled in for an exciting evening of grading tests. Finishing those, I went to bed.

I awoke with a start the next morning, but all was fine. No evil jar of sauce hung over me awaiting its chance to bash my head in. I stumbled to the kitchen, turned on the Keurig, and popped in my favorite bold blend. I had the freshly brewed coffee halfway to my lips when a flash of red caught my eye. I dashed the cup to the counter and peered in at the red substance inside. *Seriously!* I pushed the Keurig aside and found an empty jar of spaghetti sauce. In my early morning stupor, I failed to notice that a jar of that sauce had been dumped into my coffee maker's reservoir. *Geez, how do I even clean this?* I rinsed out the reservoir. I was trying to push the remaining gunk out of the machine's system when I caught a flicker of movement out of the corner of my eye.

My breath caught and a chill ran down the small of my back. I pivoted, but nothing was there. My steps quickened as I checked the corners of my studio apartment. Nothing. Ending my search in the bathroom, I locked the door and splashed water on my face. *Am I going crazy?*

I took the fastest shower of my life, grabbed my satchel, triple-checked the lock on my door, and headed to the coffee shop. Armed with a super-size, bold blend and my keys splayed before me, I made it to school with no further incident, thankfully losing myself in the boring routine of my day. I'll tell you I didn't sleep much that night. Every light was on in my apartment, and for the first time, I locked the pantry.

I awoke in panic to my alarm the moment after I had fallen asleep. I crept to the kitchen. Nothing. Coffee machine reservoir-- empty. I stared at my Keurig forlornly. Not sure that I'd got all the gunk out, I passed on my cherished routine. Locking myself in the bathroom, I showered, and headed to the coffee shop. I'll tell you, I didn't know what to think. Maybe the practical joke—if there was one—was over. Maybe I had had a delusional episode triggered by my father's off comment? I love my father. I had spent most of my life trying to please this stoic man, and he felt the need to go off on me about jarred pasta! *Do all fathers cause their sons mental trauma? Am I just lucky? How much caffeine can I guzzle without getting the jitters?*

My pace quickened as thoughts jumbled in my head. I pounded down the hallway to my classroom. The door was open. You see, I always lock the door when I leave. Reaching in, I flipped the light switches. Nothing. No one in my classroom. Entering, I closed the door.

Smash!

A jar hit the left side of my face as it crashed to the floor. It must have been perched on the edge of the top shelf to my left as I pulled the door shut. Sauce and glass sprayed everywhere. I giggled as I considered putting up yellow, *Caution* tape across my classroom. The brownish-red sauce resembled blood. And I knew I had been the intended victim.

"Oh Tony, are you okay?" Miss Hunkeler threw open my door and nearly crashed into me.

"Yeah, I'm okay."

"What happened?"

I pointed above to the shelf.

"What is that?"

"Spaghetti sauce."

"Why was it up there?'

"Well," I turned to look at her. "That is the question."

"You didn't put it there?"

I shook my head.

"We should do something about this! Catch the students respon—"

"Thanks, but I think I'll keep this quiet."

"You sure?"

What could I tell her? "Yes, I'm sure."

"Okay," she whispered. "I'll help you clean this up."

The rest of the day went without incident, and I headed home feeling exceptionally tired. Nudging open the door to my apartment, I paused, stepped inside, and tossed my keys on the table. Then, I felt it. A presence like a heavy hand pressing into my shoulder blade. Of course, no one was there. Dropping my satchel, I sat on my couch. I glimpsed the shadow out of the corner of my eye. It didn't dissipate when I turned my head to look at it. Strangely, my apartment felt ten-degrees cooler. The shadow, shaped like a man, slight of figure, smoking a cigar, reminded me of a gilded photograph at my dad's house. I shivered, remembering the comment, *"What would your grandfather think?"*

"Go away!"

The shadow disappeared. Shaking, I leaned back into my sofa, resting my head as I stared up at the ceiling. I can't tell you how it was possible, but the next thing I knew, it was morning.

I became a master of the one-minute shower. Throwing my satchel in the car, I climbed in and stared at a broken jar of pasta sauce smeared across the windshield.

"Okay! I get it!"

Locking the car and running inside my apartment, I called in sick, stuffed the six remaining jars into a bag, and hurried to the dumpster in the alley. Opening the lid, I pitched the first jar. It smashed with a metallic clang. Actually, I felt a bit better.

"What the hell are you doing?" Mrs. Spinelli had lifted her kitchen window and glared. "Aren't you a grown man? Why the hell are you breaking glass like a hoodlum?"

"You don't understand," I muttered.

"*I understand* bad behavior when I see it." She slammed her window.

I hung my head and looked down at the five jars in the bag. I didn't dare just *place* them in the dumpster. But, they had to go. I closed my eyes. *What would St. Anthony do?* At that moment, I felt warm and fuzzy inside as if the good saint had pity on me. Racing into my apartment, I added the boxes of penne to the bag. Gunning the car and setting the windshield blades on high to wipe away the mess, I zoomed out of the parking lot and careened down two blocks. I arrived at my destination just as an elderly man flipped the closed sign to open. I rapped on the glass. The gentleman raised an eyebrow as he opened the door.

"Here!" I thrust the paper bag at him.

"Pasta and sauce? Thank you."

I nodded and turned away. As I walked to my car, a contoured shadow on the brick wall across from the food bank caught my eye. I stopped.

"I gave it away."

I looked up and his shadow was gone.

At home, I cleaned my Keurig, and took a nap. Later, I brought in takeout from the *Blue Gondolier*, having stopped at *Al's Liquor & Spirits*, too. Clearing freshman essays from the coffee table, I placed baked ziti with *Blue Gondolier's* best homemade sauce next to a bottle of Chianti, nestled in the iconic *fiasco*, on the table. I felt the presence, but this time, it wasn't pressing down on me. Feeling inspired, I wound up my mom's music box, and it played *Volare*. I ate ziti in peace, drank my wine, and opened a pictorial guide to Sorrento and the Amalfi Coast. Lighting a taper, and watching the wax trickle down as I flipped through the pages, I saw the shade next to me and sensed the presence leaning over my shoulder, viewing glossy photos of the *Piano di Sorrento* that my grandfather would have viewed daily as a boy.

I swear to you, the next few days passed this way. Finishing the Chianti, I moved the taper to the basket bottle. As wax poured down its neck, pooling on the straw, the presence read over my shoulder and in the twinkling light, viewed the photos of his youth. He seemed content not to further threaten my life with some damn jars of spaghetti sauce. I don't want to throw shade at my dead grandfather, but seriously, his constant presence in my apartment was grating. I closed the book.

"Grandfather, this has to stop. I'm reformed. I'm embracing my heritage. And this book is really making me want to go to Sorrento. …Who knows?" I laughed. "Maybe I'll go and find an Italian wife. But, why are you still here? Can't you fly away? Return to your ancestral home, if not the great beyond?"

The shadow began to shimmer.

"Maybe you can find me a lovely Italian wife? Maybe I'll see you in Sorrento someday?"

I don't know how I knew, but the presence departed. I was alone in my apartment for the first time in a week—well, until dad showed up two hours later.

We sat drinking our decaf.

"Nice candle." He gestured to the *Chianti fiasco.*

"Dad, I don't know where to begin… I cleared out the jars of spaghetti sauce."

"I noticed."

"Yeah, well, that's not all. Remember you asked what my grandfather would think?"

He nodded.

"Dad, I think you cursed me. Grandfather showed up. Tried to kill me with those jars of sauce! Darned well nearly got me, too."

"Oh, thank God!" My father replied. "I thought he'd never leave my house."

My mug shattered on the tile. I spluttered. "*Your* house?"

"Oh, yes, since the day he died, God rest him." My father made the sign of the cross. "Why do you think I had large parties and cooked the family recipe all those years?"

"What the hell!"

"*Cara Cognatio.*"

"What?"

My father set his mug down. "Old Italian-Roman tradition. *Parentalia* was the nine-day festival to honor and feast with your ancestors or else they would haunt you with a vengeance. Then, you celebrated your living relatives with a feast, *Cara Cognatio*, a gathering of family and a celebration of love and passion for good food. *My father* celebrated it weekly, not just once a year. *Cara Cognatio* is—something he's never let me forget-- until a week ago…. Your eating your jarred sauce made your grandfather roll over in his grave."

"So you *sent* him to my apartment?"

My dad shrugged, his flushed face disappearing into the collar of his coat like a turtle. "So," he lifted his mug. "Where is your grandfather now?"

"I think he's finally flown to Sorrento to choose an Italian wife for me."

Dad's cup shattered on the tile, now a larger flow of decaf pooling on the floor.

I grabbed a dishcloth.

"You might want to rethink that plan. You sent him to the one place in the world to which he always wanted to return. If he finds you a wife, you'll never know a moment's peace."

"The one place he's always wanted to go?"

My dad nodded.

I tell you, I prayed right then and there to St. Anthony to let my grandfather return to Sorrento and be at peace. Dad and I both made the sign of the cross. I crossed my fingers, too, just in case.

"Are you going to haunt me when you die?"

"I hope not. I really have no desire to do so."

"Good."

We cleaned up the mess and I brewed a fresh pot. We drank, and when it was time for him to go, we embraced. Dad wasn't usually a hugger. He left and I collapsed onto the couch and stared at the popcorn ceiling. The dead are supposed to leave you alone, except for the saints. Saints meddling in your life are okay. It's different. Don't ask me why.

It's been a week since my dear grandfather's departure. I've been burning the candle in the *Chianti fiasco*, reading up on Italian culture, and eating real spaghetti with my dad. (I still hate those stupid, gangly noodles.) And, I've given a wide berth to the jarred spaghetti aisle at the supermarket. But, bringing in my meager groceries, I think of the Italian wife I'll never have. It saddens me to give the boot to my aspirations of visiting Sorrento, but I'm glad to be free of my dead grandfather. Fingers crossed.

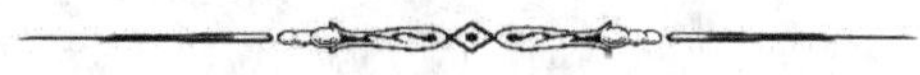

Nancy Pica Renken is a Colorado writer who enjoys reading, 'riting, and running. Her work has appeared in *Flash Fiction Magazine* and has appeared or will be appearing in anthologies by *Dragon Soul Press*, *Brilliant Flash Fiction*, *United Faedom Publishing*, *Black Hare Press*, and *Fragmented Voices*.

SUBSCRIBE!

Four issues
£22 or $30 in print
£11 or $15 digitally

www.wyldblood.com/magazine

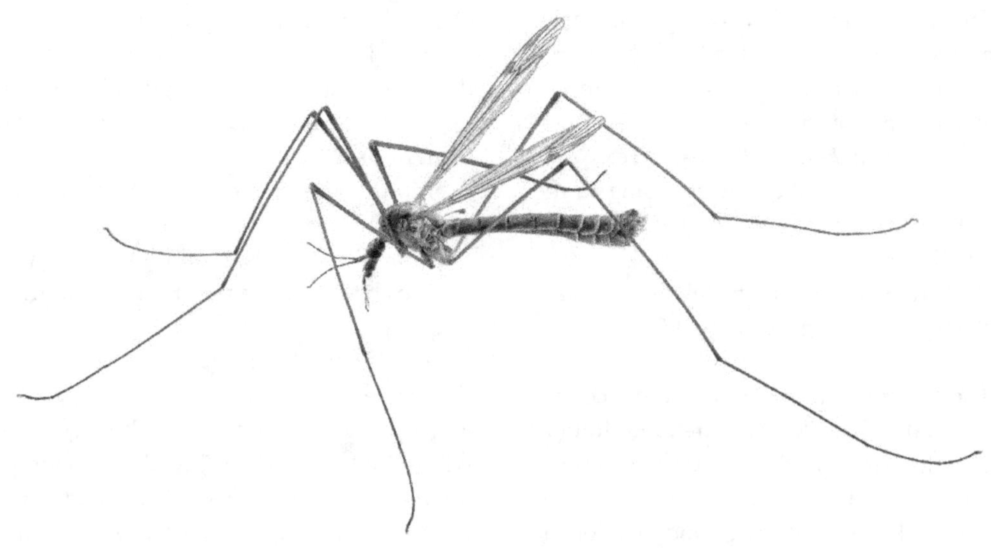

Crane Flies

JL George

September, and the grass in the top meadow is thick with crane flies. Pip dislodges them with every step and they drift into the air, limbs gangling, to swoop and flit at apparent random, threatening to dive-bomb her face or tangle in her hair.

She remembers hearing, once, that they were the most poisonous creatures on the planet, but they couldn't harm you because they didn't have mouths to bite with. Auntie Cath said that was a load of old bollocks, but then Auntie Cath was always full of it.

Always spouting old wives' tales, cautioning Pip against going near the old churchyard, or the millpond, or the crumbling stone wall in the corner of the park. Never listening to anything Pip had to say on the subject. When she's feeling charitable, Pip thinks it had to be because of her parents. They died in a car accident when Pip was a baby, and, Auntie Cath being the nearest living relative, Pip got handed off to her. Losing her sister like that, and being landed unprepared with a kid not one year old—well, it probably made Auntie Cath paranoid.

When she's not feeling charitable, she thinks Auntie Cath couldn't bear for anyone else to be right.

Annie touches her shoulder. "You alright?"

She always insists on coming along; says that's what friends are for. It's probably a good thing. Stops Pip from stewing in her thoughts the whole way up.

With an effort, Pip stops scowling and raises her face into the cold, mizzle-heavy air. "Yeah," she says, "fine."

"You don't have to keep coming up here, you know. Not if you don't want to."

Annie's looking at her sideways and, feeling uncomfortably studied, Pip does what she always does: bulldozes on through.

"Nah," she says. "'S alright. Gotta make sure the old cow's dead, haven't I?" Involuntarily, her hand goes to her raincoat pocket, feeling the curved iron weight there, rust-rough even through the Gore-Tex.

"Wouldn't you be better off going to the crem for that?" asks Annie. "They've got a plaque there."

Pip shrugs, noncommittal as she can. "Probably. But, I dunno, this just feels like the place."

They scattered the ashes up here, a couple of weeks after the sparsely-attended funeral. Trees wild-armed in the bluster, birds flung like scraps through the air high above, and Pip had to keep angling her body out of the wind to avoid getting a faceful of Auntie Cath. She was blue in the face with swearing by the time they were done, but it felt more final. More the kind of end you'd have imagined for Auntie Cath than the sedate chapel service at the crem, that was for sure. Trust that woman to be a pain in the arse even after her dying day.

"This is it, yeah?" says Annie, and Pip comes to a halt.

"Looks about right."

"None of those daddy-long-legs things up here," says Annie, peering curiously at the grass around her feet. "Thank Christ. They give me the creeps."

Pip blinks and looks down, realising she hasn't recoiled away from the erratic flight of one for ten, maybe twenty yards, though the grass up here is still long and damp enough to soak the hems of her jeans. "Yeah," she says. "Me too."

She stands and breathes in the moist air for a moment; autumn creeping closer, reaching out with chilly fingers. She takes a moment to notice it all: the wet smell of the grass, the rustle of leaves. the chatter of a sparrow in one of the browning sycamores at the fringe of the meadow. It occurs to her she's procrastinating, hesitating over the weight in her pocket for fear of—something. Of Annie thinking she's gone mental, maybe.

Scowling, she closes her fingers around the horseshoe and pulls it out. It looks dirtier up close than it did nailed over Auntie Cath's front door.

Pip's front door, now. One day she'll get used to thinking of it like that.

"Oh," Annie says, "you took it down."

Pip shrugs. "It was her thing. Thought she ought to have it."

A small lie. Too hard to explain she wants the house scoured clean of every superstition and prohibition Auntie Cath heaped on her while she lived. When she thinks about it for too long, it starts to look like a superstition in itself. And perhaps it is, because she knows she'll sleep better at night with the last of Auntie Cath's talismans discarded. Still, thumbing over the rust spots and the holes from which she pulled the age-black old nails, she imagines Auntie Cath's voice in her ear: a whisper like a shiver, like the touch of cold metal. *When we lie we poison ourselves. So you be truthful, and if you tell me fibs, I'll know. I'll see the poison in your veins, black as soot.*

"Fair enough," says Annie. Pip drops the horseshoe onto the grass with a soft thud, and that's it. They stand around, hands shoved into pockets, not saying much, and watch the trees along the sides of the meadow begin to stir in the breeze. After a few moments, by unspoken agreement, they start the long trudge back down toward the car.

There's a wind blowing up now, slanting the grass horizontal, making them both hunch their shoulders against the cold. Pip doesn't spot a single crane fly on the way back down the meadow. Hiding from the storm, she guesses. Where do they go?

She drops Annie off at the top of her street; her mum can only have the baby for so long, after all. Then it's past the shops and the rows of pebbledashed Sixties terraces to the edge of town, Auntie Cath's house posted like a sentinel against the louring hills.

Pip pulls up on the potholed driveway, watching in the rearview mirror to make sure she doesn't put her wheels into the big one on the left and damage the car. That's when she catches it: the spreadeagled outline of a crane fly on the back window.

It makes her start. Just a brief loss of control, and her rear left wheel *thunks* into the big pothole, jarring the car so hard her brain seems to rattle inside her skull. At the same time there's a horrible scraping noise, metal catching against the low stone wall that runs alongside the drive.

Swearing under her breath, she manoeuvres the car out and heads round back to check the damage, using one hand to scrape her hair back out of her face so the wind doesn't blow it into her mouth. The top of the wheel arch is scraped, but it could be worse. Nothing a spot of T-Cut won't fix. At least the tyres look fine.

The crane fly hasn't moved, though. That's weird. You'd expect it to have taken off when the car jolted, or been blown away by the wind.

With the same knot in her stomach that she always gets, being close to them, Pip leans in to take a look at it. Legs splayed, unmoving. Maybe it's dead? Or maybe not. They can go from utterly still to that random, unpredictable flitting through the air in the space of a blink. It's one of the reasons they creep her out. Nothing should be able to stay that still without being dead.

She inches closer, holding her breath, afraid to disturb the air in case she sets it off. Hard to see it properly, though, with the way the back windscreen reflects the white-clouded sky.

Wait. That reflection is smooth, uninterrupted. Pip hesitates, steeling herself, and presses the tip of her forefinger to the glass.

The crane fly doesn't move. It's on the inside.

She shudders, and decides to let it be a problem for Future Pip. Maybe it'll die overnight and she'll pick the spindly corpse off the parcel shelf with a tissue. How long do those things even live, anyway?

It's cold indoors, but then the house always is. No central heating, and the puny electric heaters that Auntie Cath grudgingly agreed to buy the winter before she died do little to take the chill off. Pip shivers, rubbing at her upper arms, and switches them all on. Even with the heaters humming away, though, the house is still too quiet, the echoes of her footsteps knife-sharp in the silence. Part of her expects to turn round and find Auntie Cath standing over her, ready with some superstitious admonishment or dire warning. It used to happen pretty regularly. She was quiet as a cat when she wanted to be.

But she's gone now. There's an extra sense of absence here today, an emptiness that lingers like a presence. A feeling like the air falling apart.

It's because of the horseshoe. Has to be. Not for any of Auntie Cath's reasons, but because it was the last piece of her left here. Pip's stripped everything else out—pulled three of them out of the fireplace, for fuck's sake. And poppets, and dusty bundles of dried herbs, and stoppered glass bottles of dirt and leaves and other things at which Pip didn't look too closely. Witch-bottles, Auntie Cath used to call them.

This town is full of bad things, she'd say. *You know a minister at St Michael's killed his wife and children? That was the badness of the town creeping in, or maybe the start of it. And when the landlady at the Lower George hanged herself in the bar, the night of the last big storm, and when Mrs Richards dropped her baby son in the millpond because she thought he was the Devil. And what happened to—well. You don't want to talk about that. The bad things can get to you, is the point, and people have forgotten how to defend against them. But not me.* And she'd lay a possessive hand against the thick stone wall. *This house will keep us safe.*

Pip snorts and forces herself to ignore the feeling. Just got rid of her—don't go turning into her.

It's around five, afternoon light filtering away and twilight gloom taking over, that she hears it. The *skrit skrit skrit* noise of a crane fly brushing against a wall or curtain, right on the threshold of hearing, so she has to turn down the telly to listen out for it.

She can't tell where it's coming from. It doesn't stop, though, *skrit skrit skrit,* and eventually she has to pause the episode of Bake Off she's watching and go hunting.

The sound's maddening, like an itch inside her ear too deep to scratch. Maybe it is inside her head, because the moment she thinks she's figured out where it's coming from and started sneaking up with the fly spray, it's behind her again.

On the verge of giving up, she gets lucky, catches the faint shadow of it out of the corner of her eye. It lights on one of the electric heaters and she swoops in, administering a good blast of the spray.

For a moment, it doesn't seem to have worked. The fly lifts into the air again, and Pip takes an involuntary step back.

It falters. Sinks, rises, sinks again—to the floor this time, where its hair-fine legs thrash and flop around, wings buzzing angrily. It takes a good few minutes to die. Pip watches it, not quite able to look away, chest inexplicably tight.

At last it stops moving, and she gathers up the soggy little corpse in a wad of kitchen roll, tosses it into the bin and washes her hands.

Skrit, skrit, skrit.

"Oh, for—" She cuts herself off, scrubbing a hand down her face in frustration, and reaches for the fly spray again.

There's a second *skrit skrit skrit* before she's found the first one, this time. How the hell are they getting in?

Eventually, Pip manages to corral them both behind the sofa, and she presses her sleeve over her nose and fills the whole space behind it with a cloud of fly spray. She forces herself not to hang around watching them die, this time, waits five minutes and comes back with the kitchen roll.

Skrit, skrit, skrit.

It has to be the chimney. The old fire still works, theoretically, though she can never be bothered to clean it, or to drive out to the Davis place on the other side of town for fuel.

First thing's first: get that covered up before she goes looking for any more of the disgusting things. She digs out an old sheet and duct-tapes it over the mouth of the chimney, searching the edges for crane fly-sized gaps with paranoid eyes. As she works, she grows conscious of the wind blowing up outside again, though it's a funny sound; a low murmuring susurrus accompanied by a scratching noise. The trees out front knocking against the windows again, she supposes. Probably need cutting back.

Some nervous gnawing at the back of her mind makes her go and check, and peer into all the bedrooms for good measure, but the windows are shut tight. Meaning the chimney's the only ventilation in the house. Probably not a good idea to go squirting fly spray everywhere, but it's that or let the crane flies win. Auntie Cath used to hang bunches of lavender and mugwort in the windows in summer to repel insects. Pip always thought it was more of her nonsense, but right now she wishes she hadn't thrown out all that stuff.

She hesitates a second and grabs the hand towel out of the upstairs bathroom. Smells a bit musty—she really must do the laundry— but she wraps it over her nose and mouth and heads back downstairs, closing all the bedroom doors before she goes.

Skrit, skrit, skrit. Despite the sheet over the fireplace, the sound seems to have multiplied in her absence, to be coming from every direction at once.

Maybe they were in here already when she came home, lurking in corners, plastered low to the stones. Waiting for her. Pip's stomach tightens and she forces the thought away. That's nonsense. Same sort of nonsense Auntie Cath would've come out with.

Pip stalks around the living room, the kitchen, the downstairs loo and the lean-to where the fridge and washing machine stand. Nothing but that infernal little noise.

She's going in circles, making herself dizzy, and the towel wrapped around her face makes her breathing feel too hot and close. Claustrophobia presses in on her. Something insubstantial brushes her ear, an insect-whisper of wings and legs, and she lets out an undignified noise, too high and loud for a grown woman to make over a *fly* of all things, and drops the spraycan. It goes spinning away across the floor.

Skrit, skrit, skrit. And oh, of course, *now* she can see them. One in the corner of the ceiling. One near her foot, so that she shudders and shies back. One lands delicately and, it seems, quite deliberately, on the spraycan and stays there, unmoving.

Fuck this. She needs to get outside. A bit of fresh air, a respite from all that flyspray floating around in here—that's what she needs. Then she'll come back and sort it out.

Pip makes for the front door, dodging crane flies, shoving her feet into her shoes and not bothering to tie the laces. Before she gets there, though, she stops in her tracks.

The window in the front door is covered up, as though a translucent grey curtain has been drawn across it. For a moment Pip tells herself that it's the gloom, the storm outside bringing in black clouds. But then she registers that the curtain is moving, and it becomes impossible to pretend anymore.

It's *crawling.* Breath catching in her throat, she creeps closer. A carpet of crane flies covers the window, all of them creeping over each other, lifting off and flitting away and landing again in an endless churn.

They've come from the meadow, some part of her thinks, wildly. Auntie Cath's horseshoe was the last thing keeping them away, and when I took it up there, it drove them out. Drove them here.

Caution abandoned, she runs to the kitchen window. The light in the room is muted and grey, and she knows before looking that it's the same. The living room, too, and all the windows upstairs.

She thinks about barricading herself in; heads to the living room, registering vaguely that the towel's fallen from over her face and she doesn't know where she dropped it.

The blanket she taped over the fireplace is coming loose, one corner flapping, useless as the carcass of an umbrella abandoned during a storm. And spindle-legs are creeping out from behind it.

Pip turns, runs upstairs, stumbling over her own feet. She slams down on one knee, the worn carpet burning her palms as she catches herself, and has to force herself upright again, hobbling the last few steps to the landing. Behind her, *skrit, skrit, skrit.* Multiplying, becoming a buzz, a chitter. She almost doesn't dare look toward the sound.

But look she must. It's a cloud of them, drifting toward her, and in a mass they seem to have purpose, all that random, unpredictable flitting making slowly but surely in her direction.

Pip opens her mouth to scream, and everything turns grey.

She wakes to motion, the sway of a car changing lanes on the dual carriageway at the edge of town. A grey, autumnal day, leaves swirling in the wind. Going to be stormy.

There's a baby in the backseat, dressed in a yellow babygro with a letter 'P' stitched clumsily onto the front. A man driving; she can't see much of him, just the reflection of bespectacled brown eyes in the rear-view mirror. And a woman beside the baby, occasionally glancing up from her book with a small smile to check on her child. At the sight of her, Pip's heart almost stops. She knows that smile, though more from photographs than memories. It's her mother.

She hears it, then. Skrit, skrit, skrit.

In the mirror, she sees the man—her dad—frown. "Em?" he says. "What's that noise?"

Her mother sets the book down. "Don't know. Nothing wrong with the car, is there?"

"I bloody well hope not. Only got the MOT done last week." He pauses. "At least they threw out that stupid doll-thing your sister insisted on hanging off the mirror. We can do without her superstitious nonsense."

Her mother's not listening, peering around the interior of the car. "I can't see anything."

Pip can sense it, though. She can see it, swooping one way and another, making its way at last to the baby. To her. It lights, ever so gently, on her face.

Her baby-blue eyes snap open, and she opens her mouth and lets out a banshee wail that drowns out the howling of the wind.

The car swerves. Her father swears. There's a huge moan of wind as he fights for control of the steering wheel, and then all is breaking glass and twisted metal.

A moment's silence, and baby Pip starts to scream again.

She's standing at the side of the road, now, looking down at the wreck. She doesn't want to see it but she can't seem to turn away.

A hand finds her shoulder, breaking the trance, and she blinks and spins toward it. It's Auntie Cath, her hair pinned up into the familiar grey-streaked bun, the St Christopher she always wore glinting at the neck of her blouse. Her face is softer than it ever was in life, but Pip still braces for the I-told-you-so.

Instead, Auntie Cath sighs. "I'm sorry," she says, very gently, and takes Pip by the hand.

They find her two days later, when Annie gets worried by the lack of replies to her texts and sends her husband up to check. The TV is still on pause, Prue Leith's face frozen in a grimace over an unappetising quiche, and Pip is lying on the landing.

Poisoned herself with flyspray, says the coroner's report. It was everywhere in the house, all the windows shut and a sheet pinned over the fireplace, though nobody can figure out why. After all, the old stone house has stood for centuries never troubled by so much as a kitchen mouse, and though they check every room, there isn't an insect to be seen.

JL George lives in Cardiff and writes weird and speculative fiction. Her work has appeared in Fireside, Cossmass Infinities, Curiosities, and various other magazines and anthologies, and her first novel The Word will be published by New Welsh Rarebyte in October. In her other lives, she's a library-monkey and an academic interested in literature and science and the Gothic.

Goldilocks and the Department of Facts

Kathy Gollan

As the new girl comes towards us, striding out on high heels, her umbrella doggedly following behind, I wonder how Jeremiah would have handled it. If he were here. She's a nobody, a transfer from the regional office, and she's going to show us all up, apparently. Her manager says her work is brilliant, the best he's ever seen. He thinks she's too much of a loner, but I'm used to that; all the Facticide Officers have their little quirks. Given what we do it isn't surprising; disappearing facts is vital and dangerous work and not something you can brag about at a dinner party.

She's cute, in spite of her curly hair, which to me is a sign of a brain at risk of curdling. I turn to Ranjit, to see if he agrees with me but he's off on his own grumbly riff. 'What's with the Miss Goldilocks thing anyway? What does that even mean? Her hair isn't yellow. And it takes too long to say.' Ranjit's a man in a hurry.

I glance over at the Apprentice, in case her name means anything to him, but his eyes are attached to his shoes.

She's here. The umbrella catches up to her and presses against her hip, as if seeking shelter from the harsh lines of this big city. She absentmindedly strokes its handle. Smiling brightly at Ranjit instead of me she says, 'Reporting for duty, sir. Facts, be my enemy!'

It's moments like these that I most feel Jeremiah's absence. Under the warmth of her greeting he would have uncurled himself to his full height, given her one of his own blazing smiles and borne her off in a cocoon of fascinating insider talk. I've seen him do it countless times. He enjoyed the hugger-mugger of people, unlike the rest of us. Which makes his disappearance doubly baffling.

But he's not here and I am, so I do my best, pretending not to notice her embarrassment when she realizes that I'm the one in charge, not Ranjit. I show her around the office, with its shabby walls and try-too-hard carpet. The chairs, excited by someone new, are crowding around her, getting in the way. Furniture everywhere has developed some consciousness since the Theory was discovered, but in most places it's limited to a slight skittishness. In our office the chairs have little personalities, bumbling and friendly but irritating. Like a dog pushing its muzzle into its owner's hand they have no sense of personal space. I tell Goldilocks we're thinking of asking the Department of Inanimates to get rid of them, but there's no guarantee the replacements will be any better.

I introduce her to her new colleagues; there's Berta, raw-boned, angry, with red hair that she winds into a knot behind her head. A Wailer in her spare time. Ranjit, handsome, nervy. The Apprentice is hugging a corner and tapping his pencil thoughtfully against his teeth as if he can't decide whether to write to the new girl or eat her. The rest of them, a motley crew.

We're struggling through the small talk when she asks abruptly, 'When is Director Jeremiah coming back, sir?'

'In his own good time, no doubt,' I say, a bit testy.

Her eyes skittering around the room as if she suspects us of hiding Jeremiah in a cupboard, Goldilocks says, 'He said I could visit the Scientists. I know they're in a detention centre, but he said he'd try and get me in. We were talking about how they weren't to blame. They didn't know what the Theory of Everything would do, they thought it was just a way of describing the universe. I wanted to ask them about that.'

I swallow hard. It was treason to talk like that. But Jeremiah could have encouraged her, just to stir things up.

'The Scientists should have known,' Berta interrupts savagely, 'it's their job to know. But no, they discover the Theory, and suddenly the world is clogged up with facts and everything's semi-alive. It's alright for you, for us, facticide is part of the solution. But some people can't cope when their brains fill up with facts. Brain-curdling, you should know about that, even where you come from.' Startled, Goldilocks gathers her umbrella protectively towards her, and drops the subject. I make a note to tell her about Berta's husband, how his brain curdled and then he ran away to live with wombats in the bush. Even in winter he wouldn't come home.

I hurry them off to the special morning tea, where all our celebration staples, seaweed, jelly snakes, carrots and mushrooms are laid out on the table. The cups sidle off the saucers and gather in a huddle as far as possible from Berta, who seems to frighten them even more than she does the rest of us.

We finish morning tea by singing the Department song. Goldilocks has a clear, high voice and knows all the words. We dribble through the last lines .... *When knowledge retreats, when facts disappear. Then hope will return and minds can be clear. In the service of ignorance, of ignorance, our Department stands strong, stands strong ...* and everyone scuttles back to their desks, relieved that the socializing is over for the day.

Over the next few weeks we're all on our best behaviour as we rearrange ourselves around the new girl. No-one comments on Goldilocks' country clothes, or the umbrella following in her footsteps or even her strange name. No-one tries to call her Goldie. The Apprentice, a gawky, long-limbed boy, hovers around her like a miasma. For the first time I notice he has a smile that lights up his face. She tolerates him but it's clear she's impatient for Jeremiah to return. I don't tell her what he said to me as he slipped out into the night the last time I saw him. 'Dream big baby,' he said, and punched me on the arm. I scoffed at the time because it was a joke between us that he was the dreamer, the one with the big ideas, and I was the process guy who made it all happen. For me it was about the rules and regulations, he loved to push the limits. We were a good team. But now he's gone off following who-knows-what dream, and I have to keep everything on track.

I take Goldilocks out on a field trip to show her the head office protocols for fact hunting. We stalk the streets, stones and little creatures scuttling out of our way, raindrops following behind us. I soon find out how she got her reputation. She's the best I've seen at tracking down the databases. They don't want to be eviscerated, understandably, so they hide in any nook and cranny, in pipes and drains. But Goldilocks is like a truffle dog, she has an uncanny ability to sense the thickening of atmosphere that shows they're nearby.

We all know how to deal with them once they've been found. It's the thrill of our work, to take a complete, bloated database, and disappear its information. It's as though we are rubbing out the answers in a completed crossword, making spaces for future generations to fill in. I watch as Goldilocks, handling the heavy extraction tongs as if they were tweezers, whips out the facts and vaporates them, neatly, humanely, no mess. It's facticide as art. False facts, which the rest of us find distracting and mind sapping, don't seem to slow her down at all. When she's finished with a database the gaps are perfect, like a Swiss cheese where the holes are more tasty than the cheese itself.

If anything, she's too enthusiastic. We've unearthed a quantum database, messy and unstable as they always are, and before I know it, she's emptied it out completely, leaving nothing, no clues, no suggestions, nothing to build on. Even Schrodinger's Cat is gone forever, until someone else, probably not called Schrodinger, reinvents it.

Back at the office, I pull her into line. 'You can't take out everything, just because you can, there's a list, there's a process. You've got to follow the rules. Otherwise there'll be chaos. Again.'

'Follow the rules?' Her eyes widen, as if it had never occurred to her that someone of her talent and beauty could be bound by the rules.

'Yes, even you. The rules are all we've got.'

As I'm speaking, Ranjit appears in the doorway. Like the Apprentice, but more discreetly, he always seems to be where Goldilocks is.

'Ah yes, the rules. Very important. Do you remember,' he says to me, 'when Ignorance is Bliss was active? That anarchist group? No rules for them.' He turns to Goldilocks. 'Their answer to the Theory? Wipe the slate clean so we could start all over again, simple as, knowing nothing. Do it better next time.'

I shudder, a chill passing over me as I remember the group and the seductive purity of their vision. But Goldilocks is fascinated, leaning forward on the edge of her chair like a racehorse under starter's orders. 'Knowing nothing....' she murmurs.

'Yes, they went on about an Ignorance bomb,' Ranjit says, 'a bomb that would send us back to the Stone Ages. Make our job redundant.'

'They were dealt with and they're gone I'm pleased to say,' I tell Goldilocks, 'But you can see why our work is so important. We're rolling back the Theory, but step by step, just far enough, no further. We have to know when to stop.'

Now that she has our attention, she returns to her favourite subject, the missing Director. 'About Director Jeremiah, sir', she says, 'do you think he's passed over, he's got something going, over the Styx?'

I make some conventional negative noises, trying to hide my shock. It hadn't occurred to me. Jeremiah had a high opinion of his abilities but even for him that would be reckless. Passing over is popular, there's a monthly parade for successful applicants, but coming back is difficult. Very difficult.

I'm keen to change the subject, so I invite her to come with me to visit the Ancients. 'You can ask them anything you like. They're like a database, but more bad-tempered.'

The Ancients are kept alive as a record of pre-Theory times, in secure but comfortable quarters on the edge of town. Goldilocks and I find them sitting in the sun around a table, like so many wrinkled, liverish sausages. I introduce Goldilocks to them, and they look briefly surprised but don't say anything. She is excited to meet them and wants to know all about how they lived in the olden days, with doubts and not-knowing, and what schools were for and were they frightened.

They make an effort to answer her, charmed by her interest and her green eyes, but everyone is soon struggling. They've never understood that the Theory of Everything led to all facts being known, so her questions make no sense to them. They aren't happy that children don't go to school any more, and that leads on to all the other things they're not happy about.

Then the oldest one, Raelene, flings out her hand to make a point and knocks one of their ornaments off the table. It's a china horse, much loved, which now has a broken leg. They start shouting at each other about whose fault it is, until all at once they stop and there's silence. A lawnmower murmurs in the distance.

Suddenly Raelene says, 'Well then, Miss Goldilocks, where's that Mr. Poppa Bear? And Mumma Bear?' They all giggle and shift about in their chairs.

The nurse tells us our time is up, but as I leave, I offer to take the little horse to get its leg fixed.

'It's only an ornament,' says Raelene sulkily.

I'm always surprised at how deaf the Ancients are to the feelings of inanimates.

The next week I bring back their horse, which proudly walks around the table on its new leg. The Ancients are cheerful for once, helpfully rummaging around in their old brains in answer to my questions. I ask them about the Poppa and Mumma bears they joked about on my last visit. What they say makes me dizzy with surprise. It changes everything.

I tell the driver to take the long way back to the Department, because I don't want to face what's coming. But even with dawdling we get there eventually. I send the Apprentice to find Goldilocks, and call Berta and Ranjit into my office.

'I've discovered what her name means.' I tell them.

They look at me blankly.

'There used to be a fairy story about a girl with her name. Goldilocks. And there were some talking animals, bears, they lived in a house in the forest. One day they went out and the girl called Goldilocks came to the house and ate their food.'

'I don't know this story,' says Berta slowly. 'That's impossible.'

'No-one knows this story,' I say, 'only the Ancients. It's disappeared.'

We are all silent as it sinks in. If no-one has ever heard of the girl and the talking bears it can only mean one thing – someone has disappeared a complete story, without permission.

There's a tapping at the door and the Apprentice, shiny with excitement, ushers Goldilocks in, her loyal umbrella following behind.

Ranjit doesn't waste any time on niceties, 'Goldilocks,' he spits, 'you stole a story, you stole your name. How did you do it? And how did you think you could get away with it?'

She gives a faint shrug. 'I didn't think about it. It was an experiment. It worked.'

'But it's not allowed. I didn't know it was even possible. You've taken a story,' I take a deep breath to make myself slow down, 'it's not a fact, it's not a piece of information. A whole story! It's how children learn to make sense of the world. You don't have the right to steal their stories. That girl, those bears, they're not yours to keep.'

She's frowning at the carpet, as if it holds the answer to some unasked question.

'Anyway, Jeremiah...' she says, then stops

'Jeremiah what?'

'Nothing. It's nothing.'

I warn her there will be consequences, and send her home.

'She's got to go,' says Berta. 'She's a thief and a liar.'

'No,' Ranjit disagrees, 'it's better to have her inside the tent pissing out than outside the tent pissing in.'

'That doesn't work for a woman,' says Berta, unnecessarily. They glare at each other, and then at the Apprentice, who seems to have stopped breathing in an attempt to make himself invisible.

I think quickly. 'We'll keep her, but on a short leash. She's too good to lose.'

I start the process of reviewing all her work, but the higher-ups aren't happy. If a story can be disappeared then the rules have to be rewritten, and heads will have to roll. Goldilocks is demoted and sent back to her regional office, and I'm cut adrift, sent on leave, while Ranjit is put in my place. It's a bitter pill to swallow. I pass the time walking the streets, soothing myself by reciting prime numbers. I tell the trees about the new girl who thought the rules didn't apply to her, leaving me to pay the price. A sympathetic young eucalypt shivers a puff of lemon scented air over me.

I'm allowed to go on one last official duty, the monthly Passing Over parade. Just as some people try to escape by living as animals, others want to leave this world altogether. Since the Styx appeared in a far corner of the country there's been a steady stream of applicants to go to there and cross over, taking their chances on the other side. It's the last great mystery after all. They think if the boundary between living and non-living things has blurred they can take a risk with their own life and death, assuming they can always come back if it doesn't work out.

When I arrive at the parade ground, it's overcast, with the wind sighing and whispering lies into my ears. The sermon begins with the usual prayer, begging forgiveness for what the Scientists did, with their fateful discovery of the Theory of Everything. The minister addresses the passers-over, 'You brave souls, you who are weighed down with too much knowledge, too many facts. Why not, you say, why not throw off the burden, go to the Edge, walk over the Styx to the grey beyond, see what's there?'

I stare unseeing at the passers-over standing motionless in lines in their standard issue hooded jackets. I wonder at their silent faith in what lies ahead. I wonder what the future holds for me. Then suddenly I see her in the middle of a line of passers. Hunched down, a caul covering her dark curls, it's Goldilocks. Before I know it, I'm walking out onto the parade field. My heart is thudding as I try to ignore the pinpricks of a thousand startled eyes. I take no notice of the security guard reaching for his gun and walk like Jeremiah would have, radiating authority in every step as I walk towards the podium.

'I suspect that one of your passers doesn't have the right paperwork, I need to speak to them,' I tell the minister. He looks at my Department uniform and epaulettes and indicates to the band to stop playing.

I wave Goldilocks out of the row and say quietly, while pretending to check her papers, 'Don't do this, don't go over. Without protection you can't get back. And if you do, you'll be hollowed out, a shell. It's kept under wraps but that's what happens.' I can't keep the bitterness out of my voice. Does she think her skills are that good?

'Don't worry sir, it'll be all right. I know what I'm doing,' she smiles. 'Just remember, ignorance is bliss. And it's coming.' She gives a little nod, and suddenly she's gone, back to her place in the line. I wave towards the officials as if to say I'm satisfied and the band starts up again.

I don't tell anyone where Goldilocks has gone, it's not my problem now. But one evening there's a knock on the door. It's Ranjit.

'What do you want?' In the tiny pause that follows I can see him running through his options and settling on the unvarnished truth.

'She's disappeared.'

'Yes, I know.'

'I got a message from her old office. She hasn't turned up there…. What do you mean, you know?'

I give him a small smile and go to the kitchen to fix us my special seaweed mix - smoked paprika on top.

'I saw her in the passing-over parade. She was going over the Styx, I don't know why,' I tell him.

Ranjit lowers himself carefully into a chair as if he's suddenly an old man. 'The manager said they'd prefer not to have her back anyway, she didn't fit in. He reckons she spent most of her time doing secret work for us. Did you know that?'

'No I didn't.' I say slowly, 'Was she working for Jeremiah? Why was…'

'He was testing her skills,' Ranjit interrupts, jumping to his feet. 'He'd heard she was good and he wanted to see how far she could go. He was getting her to take stories.'

'And that's why she took one for herself. Jeremiah told her it was all right. He told her she could break the rules.' I fall silent, thinking about the Goldilocks in the story, the little girl who ate all the food and broke the chair, because she was curious and that excused everything.

'So she's gone over the Styx,' Ranjit whispers. 'Do you think she's looking for him? What's he doing over there?'

'I don't know but we have to get them home,' I whisper back, 'where they belong. Where we can keep an eye on them.'

I spend the next week as if in a daze, drawing up the Recall papers with Ranjit, preparing the anticontamination suit, the brain coolant, all you would need for passing over the Styx if you are hoping to come back. We're ready to go when the Apprentice asks if he can come with us, to help with the equipment.

Finally we're ready for the journey out to the Styx. The sunflowers turn from their gossiping and watch us gravely, gazing after us as we hurtle past. The sun in an empty sky, an upturned blue saucer. Wailers trudging, Moochers dawdling, the falling sigh of crows. The peace of the countryside.

When we arrive, it's a bleak sight. There's a distant, unconcerned horizon, fences run off at angles, stopping and starting without meaning. A mist hovers just above the ground, each droplet humming faintly, like a swarm of tiny, malevolent bees. 'It looks like the earth is flat here,' murmurs Ranjit. The passers-over are gathered around a single twisted tree, one or two people patting themselves as if to say goodbye to their familiar bodies.

We watch as they hand over their papers and walk out onto the Styx, whose black sands moan and heave. Drops of silver metal like tears are tumbling to the surface, falling back. The passers, intent on keeping their step, hardly seem to notice as their clothes drop away, their hands and feet become transparent, then their whole body, until they vanish altogether.

Suddenly the Apprentice turns to me. He's quivering with tension as he says urgently, 'I want to go over. It has to be me. I know where she is, she told me. And I'm so much faster than you. I know exactly what to do, I've worked it out. I'll grab her and come back.'

I hesitate a fraction too long before rejecting his offer. I'm explaining why it can't be him when he grabs the papers and the suit from me and runs straight onto the Styx. High-stepping on his long, thin legs, he looks ungainly but he's more sure- footed than the others and passes them quickly. About halfway across he slows, looks back in our direction, then speeds on faster than ever. Then disappears.

We argue half-heartedly about following him, but our courage has leeched away in the mist. We reassure each other that he might succeed, and lead them both triumphantly back over the Styx, chastened after their adventure. But it's a fantasy. We stand about in the misty air all day, and the next, the Apprentice doesn't return. Then the time comes when we have to go back to the city. It's a long, silent trip. The sunflowers lean away from us, and the crows call insults, but I take no notice. I'm thinking about Jeremiah and his next move, now he has the skills of Goldilocks and the speed of the Apprentice at his command. I wonder if it was inevitable that his restless intelligence and his big dreams would lead him into the embrace of Ignorance is Bliss. How could I not have seen it?

There's nothing to do now but wait. The prime numbers are with me all the time now, solitary friends that I keep close to me, for fear of losing them forever. But numbers can't give me the answers I need. What will happen when they come with the Ignorance bomb? How will it be to know nothing, to start all over again? And will we do it better the next time?

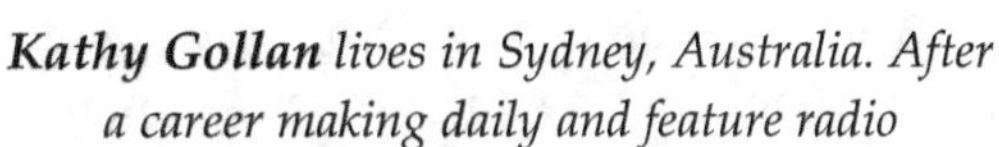

Kathy Gollan lives in Sydney, Australia. After a career making daily and feature radio programs she is enjoying the freedom of fiction

Supply, Demand and Armageddon

Michelle Ann King

I was working on Nebula's database when my father walked into the lab, accompanied by a woman I didn't know. 'Remi, have you got a minute?' he said.

Before I could say 'No,' my phone chirped, announcing the arrival of another email.

'More fan mail?' he said, giving me an enquiring smile.

I briefly closed my eyes. Fan mail. God help me, fan mail.

Marketing had recently decided we all needed to have photographs on the company website, and since I'd missed the deadline for providing a picture, my father had helpfully done it for me — which meant the Calden International *About Us* page now included a picture of me from my holiday collection, wearing a strapless yellow sundress.

'What?' he'd said, when I objected. 'It's a nice picture. Most of the others look like mug shots.'

I'd had a replacement photo taken the next morning, at a booth in the station. It looked exactly like a mug shot. I sent it straight to the web team, but apparently there was a queue for updates.

My phone chirped again.

'You know that's a compliment, don't you?' he said, reading over my shoulder. 'It's an American way of saying *attractive*.'

'I know what it means,' I said, deleting the message. Phone screens are so touch-sensitive it's hard to stab at them with any force, but I tried my best.

He shook his head sadly. 'For someone who's supposed to be interested in people's feelings, you have a very anti-social attitude.'

Stab. Chirp. Stab.

'I *am* interested in people's feelings,' I said. 'The composition and construction of emotion is fascinating. Actual people, however, tend to be a pain in the arse — which is why I work with robots. And speaking of work, I've got a lot to do, so…'

I tried to shoo him towards the door, but he didn't move.

'I want to introduce you to Vania Lisle,' he said, indicating the woman standing next to him. 'She's done a lot of music videos, as well as that wonderful web-series about the clockwork dragon. It was very popular among the under-fives.'

The woman stepped forward and smiled. She was tall, with sharp cheekbones, blue-black hair and a huge carry case slung over her shoulder. 'It's nice to meet you,' she said.

I shook her outstretched hand, feeling a little mystified. My father had brought people to the lab before, but they were usually the kind of people who worked with spreadsheets and calculators, not clockwork dragons. 'Remi Calden. I'm pleased to meet you, too.'

Nebula trundled out from behind me, whirring softly. 'And I am Nebula,' it said, angling a sensor lens up at Vania. 'Judgement regarding pleasure level of meeting currently reserved pending further data.'

Vania stepped back, almost tripping over her own feet. 'Dear God, what the hell is that?'

'Oh, don't worry,' my father said smoothly, taking her elbow. 'That's not the model we'll be featuring on the show.'

'Show?' I said. 'What show?' I looked from him to Vania. 'What's going on?'

He cleared his throat and brushed a speck of something invisible off his sleeve. 'What I need you to remember, Remi, is that this is a business. A commercial enterprise, not an academic one. Which means all departments, including yours, have to undergo a regular review of their cost-benefit ratios and practical applications in the marketplace. And after reviewing the Nebula project, I've determined a need for some directional changes.'

'I see,' I said, then shook my head. 'No, actually, I don't. What does that mean?'

'It means you need to start making money. I've hired Vania because we've identified an opportunity to increase our appeal to an important target demographic, which we can then leverage into creating a reputation for the company as a provider of innovative, interactive social entertainment, while creating advance demand for the merchandise.'

I ran this sentence through my head a couple of times, but failed to make any sense of it. 'Sorry, but you're going to have to translate that one, too.'

He let out an impatient sigh. 'She's going to help you create a series of promotional features that will publicise a new range of high-quality interactive entertainment products.'

Finally, I got it. 'Toys.'

'Exactly, yes. There's tremendous potential in this robot of yours, Remi. It demonstrates a level of interactive responsiveness that beats everything else currently on the market. All the kids will want one.'

He peered down at Nebula. 'Well, not one like this, obviously. The commercial versions will be much more attractive. Disproportionately large eyes, that's the key. People go ga-ga for big googly eyes. It's an evolutionary thing. Babies, kittens, koalas… it's why everyone loves them.'

Nebula whirred. 'I am an autonomous psycho-mimetic robotic research unit,' it said. 'I am not a toy.'

'And I'm a scientist,' I added. 'Not a kids' TV presenter. The answer's no, Dad. Absolutely not.'

'Now, Remi, I know you don't mean that.'

'I can assure you I—'

'I know that because if you *did* mean it, I'd be forced to remind you that although you're my daughter and I love you, you're also an employee of Calden International and therefore contractually obliged to perform such work or assignments as are deemed necessary. Should you refuse such an assignment your contract becomes subject to termination, with all intellectual and physical properties associated with your projects reverting to sole ownership of the company. And I know you wouldn't want to make me say something like that, would you?'

This time, I managed the translation on my own. Moral of the story: always check the small print, even when it comes to family. Even? Especially.

'*Would* you, Remi?'

I sighed. 'No, Dad.'

He patted my shoulder. 'Good girl. Okay, Vania, over to you.'

She'd been setting up a lighting rig on a tripod, and now took a hand-held camcorder out of the carry case. 'Great. I thought we could start with—'

She broke off as Nebula extended a metal sensor arm that sent the camcorder flying out of her hands, then crashed into the tripod and tipped it over.

'What the hell?' Vania said.

The camera and lighting rig hit the floor, and Nebula immediately started rumbling over the top of them. 'Mobility problem detected. Sensors indicate presence of foreign particles in internal gears. Control of motor functions inhibited.'

Something inside the camera popped explosively. Nebula made a sound that could have been the word 'Oops,' then powered down.

My father shook a piece of shattered glass off his shoe. 'I'm so sorry,' he said to Vania. 'I'll send someone out to replace your equipment straight away. Out of my daughter's budget, naturally.'

He fixed me with a glare. 'Whatever just happened, make sure you fix it before we go into mass production. We can't take the risk of kids losing control of their models like that. The liability exposure would be horrendous.'

He strode off, yelling for his PA, while I lifted Nebula onto the workbench.

'Do you want to tell me what that was about?' I asked.

An antenna poked through the access panel. 'Foreign particles in—'

'The gears, yes. So you said. Except you don't *have* any gears.'

The antenna withdrew. 'Initiating diagnostics. No communication possible while scan in progress. Please hold.'

There was a loud click, and it began to play Vivaldi's *Four Seasons*.

Vania grabbed my arm. 'This project,' she said, frowning deeply. 'Nebula. What exactly is it about? What are you trying to do?'

'I'm trying to create an algorithmic-based, non-organic analogue of the mammalian limbic system in order to replicate the informational processing of human emotional responses.'

She blew out a breath. 'Suddenly, I see the family resemblance. Could you try that again in English?'

I thought about it. 'I'm trying to develop a machine that understands feelings.'

She gave me a look I couldn't read. 'A robot that *feels*?'

'No. Machines can't have emotional experiences the way we can. But what they can do is learn to recognise, interpret and react to them. A computer, after all, is basically just a very powerful, very fast, analysing machine. So Nebula uses an intricate array of sensors to capture information — microexpressions, skin lividity, pupil dilation, eye movement, speed of heartbeat, posture, all the empirical data it can get hold of — collates it, feeds it into a specialised database, then analyses that data and compares it to previous results in order to extrapolate context and calculate an appropriate response.'

Vania rubbed her forehead. 'Okay. I think I get it. So after Nebula observed and interpreted the situation here, she calculated that destroying my camera was the appropriate action to take.'

I rubbed the back of my neck. 'Yeah, okay, fair point. Clearly, I still have a way to go yet. There must have been some kind of glitch, so—' I stopped, because she was giving me a strange look. 'What?'

'I wasn't being sarcastic. I meant what I said — she thought it was the right thing to do, in the circumstances. Don't you see?' She searched my face. 'No. You don't, do you?'

I shook my head.

'I think you *have* achieved your goal.' She let out a tiny snort of laughter. 'The robot seems to have more emotional insight than either you or your father, anyway.'

Was it pity, that look? Wonder? Both?

'The robot was trying to stand up for you, Remi. You were being railroaded into something you didn't want to do, so she tried to get you out of it by sabotaging the shoot.'

'Oh,' I said. That actually did make sense. 'If you're right, then… well, that's great. That means it was able to—'

Vania gripped my arm again, tighter. 'No, it's not. It's not great at all.'

'Ow. What? Why? What do you mean?'

Now the look was definitely disbelief. 'Seriously? Have you never watched a single science fiction film in your entire *life*?' She shook her head. 'I've seen this story before, Remi, and it doesn't end well.'

I laughed. 'Come on. We're talking about a piece of research equipment, not a… a dalek, or whatever. Nebula doesn't want to take over the world.'

'Maybe, maybe not. But either way, could you say the same for your father?'

I thought about that. 'Probably not, but what's that got to do with it?'

'He doesn't realise what you've done either, yet. But he will. And then it won't be supermarkets and toy shops he'll be trying to sell these things to, it'll be foreign arms dealers, the intelligence services and the military-industrial complex. And you know what happens after that, don't you? We all end up living in an Arnold Schwarzenegger film.'

'I haven't actually seen many Schwarzenegger films,' I said. 'I'm more of a Liam Neeson fan.'

Vania gave me that look again. 'That *really* wasn't the important part of the analogy.'

'No, okay. Sorry. But…' I shrugged. 'I'm not sure what you want me to say.'

'How about that you'll stop developing technology that could lead to the utter annihilation of the human race?'

My phone chirped. *Mail received*, the notification said. *From: A Fan. Subject: Hi, Sexy!!!*

I looked back at Vania. 'Can I think about it?'

She started to say something but was cut off by my father barreling back into the lab with his PA, who was laden with boxes of new camera equipment.

'Here you are, girls,' he said, smiling bountifully at Vania. 'Take your pick, and we can get back on schedule.'

'I'm sorry, Mr Calden,' Vania said. 'Remi was just telling me that the Nebula model is broken beyond repair. We won't be able to use it at all. For anything. Ever again.' She gave me a piercing look. 'Isn't that right, Remi?'

'Well—'

My father shrugged. 'It won't make any difference, we weren't going to be using that one anyway. It would have given the kids nightmares.' He scooped Nebula off the workbench and thrust it into the arms of his PA. 'Jamie, get rid of this, will you?'

'Oh,' I said, holding up a hand. 'Ah. Er—'

Jamie stopped and looked back at me with an enquiring expression. 'Yes, Remi?'

Vania stood on my foot, grinding the heel of her boot into my toe.

I dropped my hand. 'Nothing. It doesn't matter.'

Vania smiled brightly. 'Great. Let's get back to the show, then. Remi, why don't we start with you explaining how everything the robots do is governed by remote control and pre-programming, and how very, very far away you are from developing anything close to true autonomy?'

'Good idea,' my father said. 'Here, you can demonstrate with one of the new models.'

He handed me a white, gleaming robot that looked a bit like a koala. It blinked big, disproportionately large eyes at me and declared, 'I love science!'

He looked at his watch. 'Right. I'm going into a conference with Marketing, so send me the video when you're done, and I'll run it past the focus group.'

He left the lab as Vania set up her new camera and hoisted it to her shoulder. 'I'll need some background footage for the credits sequence,' she said. 'I'm thinking of a time-lapse idea, show the progression from spec drawings to circuit boards to finished product, that kind of thing — you must have some old stuff lying around, from the early stages?' She looked around, then headed for the door at the rear of the lab. 'Is this a storage room? Have you got anything like that in here?'

'Ah, no. That's not — Vania, wait. You really don't want to go in there,' I said, but she'd already opened the door.

The robots inside all stopped and swivelled their sensors towards her. 'Hello,' said the nearest. 'I am Nebula Two. Pleased to meet you.'

Another scuttled forward. 'I am Nebula Seventeen. Greetings.'

'Hello,' said a third, bumping her foot. 'I am Nebula Eighty-Four. New research subjects—' it paused, whirred, then continued, 'new friends are always welcome.'

'You appear pale and somewhat shaken,' said Nebula Seventeen. 'This is possibly symptomatic of low blood sugar. Would you like a biscuit?' The metal panel in its midsection opened, and a plate of chocolate Hob Nobs slid out.

'Hey,' I said, as Nebula Forty-Three circled behind her and extended an extraction unit. 'No collecting DNA. I've told you, that's rude.'

Nebula Forty-Three retracted the unit with a snap. 'Apologies.'

I offered Vania a tentative smile. 'They mean well, honestly. They're just not quite as well-socialised as the original.'

'Would you like to stay and socialise with us?' Nebula Eighty-Four asked. 'We like to watch Arnold Schwarzenegger films.'

'Thank you,' Vania said faintly, edging away. 'That's very kind of you. But I really have to go now.'

She backed up slowly until she reached the door, then turned and fled.

'Come back soon,' called Nebula Two, but she was already gone.

My father dropped by the lab a couple of hours later, to tell me Vania had quit. Her agent had called to say she'd decided to give up film-making in favour of running post-apocalyptic survival training courses.

'Strange career choice,' he mused. 'I wonder what could have brought that on?'

'I have no idea,' I said.

'Although…' He was checking something on his phone. 'It looks like there's money in it. Not just training courses, but equipment too. Portable water tanks, medical kits, freeze-dried food packs, weapons, underground shelters… you know, the end of the world looks like it could be quite a profitable business.'

He carried on scrolling through the information on the screen. 'But do you know what none of these places seem to be selling? Not one?'

I shook my head.

'Robots! Just think how useful apocalypse-ready robots could be. They could explore toxic environments, repair machinery, perform battlefield surgery, kill zombies… all the self-respecting doomsday preppers will want one.'

He pointed at me. 'There's a gap in the market here, Remi, and I want you to fill it.'

'What about this?' I said, picking up the koala robot sitting on the workbench. 'And the promotional videos?'

He shook his head impatiently, plucked the koala out of my hand and tossed it aside. 'Forget about toys and gadgets, Armageddon's clearly where the money is. I want you to make this your priority from now on, Remi.' He tapped at his phone. 'Okay, I'm setting up a meeting with Manufacturing to talk about production schedules. So come on, get to work, there's a good girl.'

When I didn't move, he frowned. 'What? Is there a problem, Remi?'

In the pocket of my lab coat, my phone let out its *New Message!* chirp.

I shook my head. 'No, Dad,' I said. Then I opened the access panel of the nearest Nebula, and did as I was told.

Michelle Ann King is a short story writer from Essex, England. Her stories of fantasy, science fiction, crime, and horror have appeared in over a hundred different venues, including Strange Horizons, Interzone, Black Static, and Orson Scott Card's Intergalactic Medicine Show. Her collections are available in ebook and paperback from Amazon and other online retailers, and links to her published stories can be found at her website: www.transientcactus.co.uk

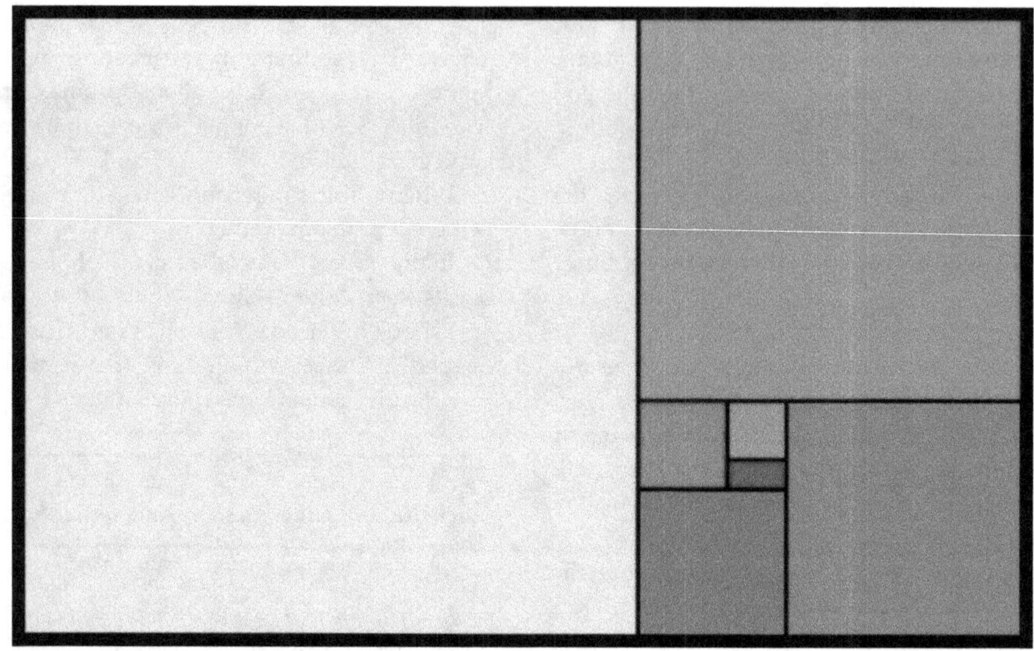

Savant

Tom Learmont

My story begins back in 2030, when the world was a safer and more innocent place. But it was still a bad year – no one will ever forget the big San Andreas shudder, the evacuation of the submerged Maldives, the crunch-gum cancer debacle, Italy's return to fascism and the Chinese upheaval. A year from Hell, with record temperatures, tornadoes, hurricanes, floods and lethal school fusillades by a dozen demented killers. Plus the leak of Putin's deathbed conversion and confession as well as that whole sad Australian thing, to say nothing of the Saudi coup, the South African coal riots, the accidental nuclear blast in Kashmir and the Spratly Islands naval skirmish.

The electorate was not preoccupied by major issues such as President Ivanka Kushner's crackdown on renewable energy. They, the people, were hunched over their phones, plugged into non-stop brain-deadening algomuzak. They were fascinated by the farce of the Trump statue unveiling in Muncie, Indiana – and Melania's second marriage. They were glued to streaming schmak-schmak shows, and the world buttock tattoo championships in Qatar. They loved spectacles such as Musk getting measured for a Mars suit, and Wall Street under water after super storm Donald, with jokers paddling kayaks past George Washington's statue. They were all wired-up 24/7, and never opened a damn book.

It was also a bad year for me. I celebrated my thirty-second birthday in a state of despair. I had been laid low by divorce. This came on top of an orchestrated, undercover twitter mail campaign by a clutch of ruthless corporate adversaries who wanted me out – because I outperformed them, and also to leave more room for bigger bonuses, further up the ladder. I didn't have the resources to fight back, especially when they deployed a pair of well-paid faux-feminist perjurettes with shrill accusations of rape. The case was thrown out of court, but I was beaten. The fake dirt stuck, and jobs were hard to find. Even old acquaintances who knew I was no rapist were PC enough to give me the cold shoulder. I was back to a gas-fuelled car, and a rented crash pad in Canarsie, the size of a shoe box. I don't know what a nervous breakdown feels like, but maybe I was having one.

One day I couldn't even muster the strength to start reading *Anna Karenina* again. And that was when Sigi Mortelman called. "Hi Theo – how's it hangin? Saw you in the yearbook and thought maybe you can give me a hand with a little project of mine. You still know how to run a business?"

"I know how to run a business, Sigi. You got a start-up or what?"

"Something like that. Wanna come over for coffee?"

His basement in Jamaica wasn't much of an improvement on my lair of despair in Canarsie, but it was a lot bigger, and even more untidy. He had a wall of racks with twinkling lights, which he explained away with a wave of the hand, saying, "Quantum it ain't – but it gets the job done." He introduced me to his friend Sophocles, clad in overalls, sitting at a table piled with papers. He was my age, I suppose – bald with a round face and a broad smile, into which he occasionally inserted a Pringle. When he wasn't fiddling with a big lump of what looked like green modelling clay.

"Sophocles – meet Theodore. I hope he's going to come and work with us."

"Hi Theodore!" He shook my hand then dug his blunt fingers back into his ball of clay.

Sigi drew me to the other end of the big room and sat me down in a bursting, tattered sofa with a hot cup of coffee. He took a chair alongside me and said, "Just to clear the air, Ted – I don't swallow that rape bullshit, okay? So how's married life?"

"Over, but with no hard feelings. We each married an illusion. Then one morning we woke up and saw each other as strangers – who were totally unsuited. It was mutual. And you?"

"Short-term serial monogamy – you know me from college, I'm too absent minded to hold a chick for long." There was always a dog-eared science fiction paperback jammed into the hip pocket of Sigi's jeans. His rocket scientist's head was so full of code and number theory that he could never remember where he was supposed to be that evening. In college, I was forever calling him with reminders of things like fencing practice or chess club meetings.

"So how's it been otherwise, Sigi?"

"Some job hopping in IT – made a bit of money. But now I've got a project of my own and I've made a small investment in it. Ted – you know how hopeless I am at organising anything except numbers. You used to keep me in line. You and I go way back, and I trust you. Now, I'm thinking maybe you can do the same for me on a bigger scale. With your corporate experience, that MBA of yours – how big a business could you run as CEO? I mean everything – bank accounts, management, staffing, hiring, firing – all that stuff?"

"Sure, Sigi. I can run a business from the top. And as the business grows, I know how to expand. I can build you a garden of forking paths, so to speak. What sort of turnover or capitalization are we talking here – millions, billions?"

Sigi laughed. "Don't talk peanuts, Ted. If you join me, we'll be back in the golden age – like Bill Gates and his buddy in the garage – but on steroids."

"Have you got a name for this juggernaut?"

"SAVANT – but that's only for the good to know."

"Okay, but what does it mean?"

He lowered his voice and looked across to where Sophocles sat with his clay. "There's an old French term: *idiot savant,* meaning wise idiot. My lovable assistant and friend over there is one. His IQ is down through the floor, but he's got a biological number cruncher between his ears." He stood up and led me over to Sophocles. "Soffy my bud – can you give me the price-earnings ratio for Unifruco at close of business on 17 September 1938?"

Sophocles momentarily stopped kneading clay and said, "Price was sixteen point three times earnings, Sigi."

"That's on the nail, Soffy. Can you show me a fibo? Fibo . . . Lessee, fibo 82, please."

Sophocles rattled it off: "Fibo 82 is 61305790721611591."

I had to look that up all these years later and copy it.

Sigi said, "But can you show fibo 82 to Ted?"

His stubby fingers worked the clay into a shape which meant nothing to me, even as a three-dimensional Rorschach. It could have been a green dog turd with amoeboid pseudopodia, perhaps. Sophocles handed it over to me. As I contemplated the weird shape, Sigi started explaining.

"Ted – that shape is how Soffy explains what he sees in his head when he calls up Fibo 82, with all 17 digits."

"But what's Fibo 82?"

"It's a number theory thing – a sequence that starts 0 -1 - 1 - 2 - 3 - 5 - 8. Fibo six is the number eight. Fibonacci numbers. As they build you add the two previous numbers to get the next one."

I handed back the cool clay blob and said, "Wow, Sophocles! You are one clever guy. I could never do that."

Sigi said, "I'm so proud of Soffy. He's my best bud, and I'll always look after him."

Back at the other end of the room, Sigi added, "There's a lot I don't understand about how Soffy does it. You know he's a cousin? Okay, when I first met him ten years ago at Thanksgiving, I read up on savants. I was fascinated. He became my legal ward, and I love the guy – he wouldn't last a minute out there without me. And here's the thing – Soffy and his clay, plus those racks and my nerdish nature are an unbeatable combination. Well, for what I hope to achieve."

"Which is?"

"To become the richest man in the world. By playing the market legally in an unsuspected, undetected way, in an environment ruled by a widely-held fallacy."

Sigi launched into an explanation of the fallacy – a concept that Artificial Intelligence, driven by Machine Learning, would outstrip human mental capacity and take over the world. He told me thousands of people seriously believed in the Singularity – when the human race would be enslaved by a culture of robots with superior intellects.

"You can't blame them," said Sigi. "We're all wrapped up in the Internet of Things. You can't even scratch your balls these days without the lamp on your night stand blasting that fact into cyberspace. And within a second, your refrigerator, family doctor, bathroom scale, toothbrush and microwave are all aware that you had an itchy scrotum – and so is Homeland Security!"

Neither of us laughed, then Sigi said, "That's what led to the fallacy that markets operate most efficiently when run by the superior intellect of AI."

"Okay, Sigi – that's the fallacy. I'm prepared to believe you if you give me the countervailing facts."

He nodded. "Here's the thing about AI – it's all algorithms and no imagination. All imitation and plagiarism. No matter how useful, it's no more than a clever stunt, an illusion, a conjuring trick. It's no more than a fortune-telling automaton on a carny midway. Tell me – when will machine learning develop algorithms for envy, nostalgia, sympathy, empathy, erotic yearnings? Now take the Russky who wrote that book you were always reading . . ."

"Tolstoy – *Anna Karenina.*"

"Okay – that guy is working with a set of circuits inside his head which were designed by evolution in a trial-and-error process that took a couple of billion years. He uses his imagination to dream up Anna, then codes her in ink on paper. He creates something from nothing, out of nowhere. And when a fellow human being scans the code marks, his optic nerves deliver Anna, alive and breathing, into the reader's brain."

"So you did read the book!"

"Yeah, well – I figured it had to have something . . . But SF it ain't, Ted."

"I'll grant you that."

"Now forget Tolstoy and consider Sophocles, who is working in an AI way with the same basic model of brain. He could no more create something from nothing than fly to the Chinese moon base. He's all algorithm, without a shred of imagination. He can only work with what he's given. And very impressive it seems, for he's running a trial and error system a lot faster than evolution ever did. But he's only playing pick and mix with things that were there already.

"Even if a telco chip passes the Turing test by successfully impersonating a human Bangladeshi call centre operator – it's all imitation and plagiarism, not creation. Just shuffling the cards. Creation's different. It takes a leap – not a googolplex of tiny trial-and-error steps, no matter how fast they are. And that leap will be impossible for robots until there's a multi-core chip that interacts directly with a human brain, running on . . . well, a sort of a shared operating system – for lack of a better term. Which could take a thousand years IMHO – if the Anthropocene doesn't burn out first. But in the meantime, most of us are in the grip of the big fallacy. D'you get my point? "

"But Sigi – surely there is danger, even if there's going to be no Singularity?"

"Right! You couldn't put Soffy in charge of the world without a whole chain of disasters."

At college, Sigi used to berate me for my lack of interest in science fiction, and he got back on his old hobby horse soon enough, talking about his hero Vonnegut, who had evidently published his first novel *Player Piano* in 1952.

"Kurt Jnr saw it all back then, when he was working for General Electric. Electronics was called automation at the time, and there were tragedies from the word go. Empathy went out the window. In *Player Piano* two old ladies starve to death in an automated rail car, because they don't know the algorithm that opens the door. That was a warning nobody heeded. Let's face it, Ted – there are disasters every day, when the world is run by a blind algorithm feeling its way ahead into the dark, using scraped-up historic data. An algorithm that's supposed to understand and control emotion, for cryin' out loud – things such as cultures of irrational hate that go back centuries, as in the Balkans and Northern Ireland. Some people expect the Singularity to write better than Tolstoy. Only non-readers could swallow that one. In any case, forget AI – aka Artificial Ignorance. But you can also forget pistol-packing stainless-steel robots with red eyes. We already have something much worse, in the shape of President Kushner."

By the time we were on the third cup of coffee, I decided I had nothing to lose. Sigi Mortelman and I had always trusted each other. He was offering me 32% of SAVANT, the same as Sophocles, while he would hold the balance. "Okay Ted – here's what we do. If you know an honest lawyer, get him to draw up all the papers. Once the company is up and running, you'll be in charge of the day-to-day affairs. It's got to be 100% private – ring fenced, with you, me and Soffy inside.

Subsidiaries can come later. Next week, take me to your lawyer – I'll introduce you to my bank. I'm giving you a measly five mill to play with, but it's probably enough to get us off the ground."

Six weeks later, the sad threadbare linen of my Canarsie hidey-hole lay far behind me. The new place in Brooklyn Heights, remodeled from one floor of a brownstone, was the coolest man cave I'd ever inhabited – the kind of place where a fellow could get his feet up on an Eames ottoman and read *Anna Karenina* to his heart's content. I was in a space where I could easily lock up and take a healthy walk across the bridge to enjoy a gourmet lunch in the Financial District with my partners.

We ate at a rooftop restaurant in an old skyscraper toward the east end of Pine Street. Soffy had brought his own Pringles. The sunny view from the fiftieth floor stretched from mid-town, across to the East River and its bridges. Almost directly below us, construction crews on barges were working on the tall new flood dyke that would run along South Street and around to the shrunken shoreline of the Battery. To keep the kayaks out of Wall Street, joked Sigi. The air above the river swarmed with drones, like mosquitoes hovering over a creek. Above them, the occasional full-sized chopper held its course up-or downstream. And the whole scene faded away into a far-off bank of clouds over Coney Island.

I had been busy. SAVANT was renting premises in Brooklyn. To assist me, I had hand picked and head hunted a COO, a CFO, a CA, a clerk, a receptionist, a website designer, an intern, a lawyer – and set up several bank accounts. I attended confidential weekly meetings with Soffy and Sigi at the basement in Jamaica. As far as I could make out – everything was 100% legit. Cash flow was reliable, and swelling to a flood, not that I fully understood how it was generated. An exclusive encrypted cloud was involved, plus an entire forest of block chains – but I had gathered that these were mere ancillaries, not the mainspring of SAVANT.

Sigi had ordered the truffle-and-shrimp duck egg omelet; I was savoring a langoustine poached in cognac. The sommelier had persuaded us to try a crisp Chilean sauvignon blanc. Soffy toyed with a saucerful of Pringles and a can of Coke Zero, much to the maitre d's silent disdain. And Sigi was giving me an informal run-down on trading algorithms 101.

"I've seen some weird ups and downs driven by machines which pile into the market – or out – based on what the other machines are doing. And guess what – every algorithm on Wall Street is a cousin to the one in the next-door outfit. They're all predictable to each other, with very similar software. Rule by such retard chips follows herd mentality. Which is a very long way from the fearsome singularity old Musk keeps banging on about. It's vital to stay a millisecond ahead of the competition, when you tap the key to place the order or cancel it. With Quantum coming in, the time gap will shrink further."

"To a millionth of a second?"

"I wouldn't say no to that, Ted. Remember, in my world there's no such thing as instantaneous . . . Not until you run up against Planck Time. And we're still a long way above that, stuck at an observational record of 820 elapsed zeptoseconds."

"Sigi – have you crashed through that barrier?"

"I wish . . . And if you're asking is that a link to the secret behind SAVANT, no. Fascinating, but of no import to us." He grinned, stole a Pringle off his ward's plate and said, "Soffy – The Giro d' Italia bike race of 1947, who won, and in what time?"

Soffy said, "Angelo Fausto Coppi, in a time of 115 hours, 55 minutes and seven seconds."

"And Soffy my bud – who was second?"

"Gino Bartali, in a time of 115 hours, 53 minutes and 24 seconds."

"And what would his time be, expressed in zeptoseconds?"

Soffy reached for his clay and he began to knead. Then Sigi's hand closed on top of the working fingers and he said, "It's okay, my brother – you don't need to tell me the result. I've changed my mind."

Soffy said nothing, but when Sigi lifted his hand, he held up his answer in the clay, which looked pretty spiky to me, with the odd little cavity and tassel. That night I couldn't get the new word out of my head. I had a dream about Soffy, who was singing: "I got the zepto-zepto-zeptosecond blues."

A year later, when SAVANT had offices in Ireland, Malta, Panama and Cyprus, my garden of forking paths was spread half way across the globe, and Sigi decided we needed a building in Manhattan. We didn't pay for a new one, which would have taken too long to erect, but took over a quality existing tower for cash, well above the flood line on the upper east side. Our private cloud was everywhere and nowhere, humming 24/7. The racks in Jamaica, NYC, were now duplicated, twinkling in Montana, far down in an old hard-rock mine. They were also cloned in various South African and Australian bunkers, linked by orbital relays. And we were getting our toes wet with Quantum.

Sigi's remark about becoming the richest man in the world had begun to seem less like an idle boast. Investment clients had been useful in the beginning, but that revenue stream was shrinking. Income from our private deals had begun to snowball exponentially, and SAVANT slowly withdrew from the big board, without

fanfare. It was my job to sprinkle our private wealth evenly on the surface of the terrestrial globe, and Sigi gave me a free hand. Just after we took over our first brokerage in '35, the triumvirate took a summer holiday in Greenland. And it was there that Sigi told me the full secret of SAVANT.

We were sitting in a glass-walled observation tunnel running through an artificially iced-up polar bear sanctuary – some 20 miles by maglev from the lawns and fruit trees of the Radisson Arctic. Soffy liked the bears, but he tut-tutted when one grabbed a seal from a hole in the ice of the lake and painted the snow red with it. The savant went back to his clay, and the earplugs which fed him info during most of his waking moments.

I told Sigi, "Your ambition is beginning to look achievable. And I'm wondering what you'll do when you get there, in a few years' time."

"It's the voyage that matters, not the destination, Ted. Tell you the truth, I've never really thought about that – I've been having too much fun getting there. Did you ever see Kubrick's old 2001 movie? At the end a star child is born, who reasons that he'll think of something to do. Maybe I'll be a bit like that – I dunno . . ."

Then he changed tack and asked, "You do a great job in running our garden of forking paths, Theodosius. You never stick your nose into my side of the business. But I'm asking: how much of my modus operandi have you worked out?"

Under the huge gray dome, the bear was tearing at what I presumed was the seal's fatty liver. Soffy was working his clay with the dexterity of Granny Hillary thumbing an antique Blackberry. Sigi's smile was quizzical.

I said, "Only in broad contrarian strokes. Firstly, the singularity fallacy and algomania divert nosy people away from your real business model. Secondly, unlike everyone else in the market, you don't give a rat's ass about getting there one millisecond early. But then there's SAVANT – you, the racks and Soffy. And that's where I run out of clues."

Sigi said, "I'm still missing a few clues myself, Ted. In the beginning, I asked Soffy a couple of market questions, and he came up with intel I could use. But once he reached the forward limit of his reading, he got all bewildered. There is no record of the future, you see. I began to study his clay models. I scanned them and made replicas with a 3D printer, I delved into topology for a couple of years, and succeeded in partially analysing some of Soffy's shapes. We got to the stage where I could hand him a 3-D model, he'd fondle it for a sec, then identify it. With a back-and-forth method plus a bit of topological software written by myself, I tied the system to a foundation of basic game theory, and we were getting 20% compounded over a two-year forward horizon."

"Sigi – don't tell me you can read the future!"

"Well, I can, actually – but only to a degree. Plenty of mistakes and surprises, but once these are weeded out, we still get our 20%, by looking two years ahead "

"How come nobody copied you?"

"We have a decoy algorithm for our few traded shares which – like every other AI machine – is hooked on microseconds. It's my way of throwing some beef to the wolves pursuing the troika. So far, it's fooled every algosniffer. They're all too greedy to work on a two-year timescale, the damned penny snatchers. And the mainsprings of our growth are concealed by private, ring-fenced nodes in your garden of forking paths."

"Sigi – you're leaving me behind with all this SF!"

"Okay – stop me if you get confused. Here's the trick. I use my topology app in the racks to edit Soffy's clays – and rewrite the data to read two years ahead of the present. When Soffy's fingers read the 3-D printouts, he gives me info which his brain interprets as past events. Then it's back to the racks, and the intel they spit out is high-probability stuff that gives us our gains in the end. We take the very safest kind of bet."

I breathed out, and said, "Tax is taken care of. All over the garden we are in compliance."

Sigi grinned. "Breaking the law is out of the question."

Ten years later, Sigi was the wealthiest man in the world, with Soffy and I close behind as a pair of runners up. He'd gone through three girlfriends, and I was still bemused by Esmeralda after seven years of marriage and two children: Sophocles and Sigismund. We had an architect friend called Justin, who'd done a fair bit of work for us, and he tipped us off about a big launch of a new mid-town building, Singularity Precinct. It had been reputedly conceived and designed by a quantum computer – without human assistance. The firm who owned the computer made this claim openly, but still accepted the massive fee they were charging the client – a big overblown Singaporean insurance outfit. They had gone so far as to invite Musk to the launch in the hope that it would open his eyes to the Singularity's benign nature.

And Musk actually turned up, in a Tesla 100-watt wheelchair. He revolved around the large scale model in the huge 12-storey atrium, peering at it closely with suspicious eyes. When I tilted my head back to look up at the skylight, all those floors above me, I felt as if I were at the lower end of a monstrous, contorted digestive tract. Sigi and Justin were discussing the design.

"What do you mean by 'blended', Justin?"

"The machine took bits of everybody – even tiny snips of Frank Lloyd Wright – and fed them into the blender to make a slumgullion of big styles. Just looking around down here I can see things that remind me of Frank Gehry, Saarinen, Hadad, Palladio, Campo Baeza – oh, and God knows who else." He broke off and nodded toward the large architectural model in the centre of the atrium.

"And Sigi – to me, the result is best summed up as a couple of dozen big concrete ocarinas piled up into a clusterfuck. An elephant-dung adobe."

Soffy seemed rooted to the spot, looking down, fumbling furiously with his clay, and I saw that he was copying the model.

"Soffy, what d'you make of it?"

"No pink numbers, no violet numbers – only brown. Sack of shit!" He flattened the clay to a disc between his palms.

Sigi winked at me, and said, "I could have told you so, Soffy my bud."

At that function, Sigi had his first symptom. He couldn't remember where he'd left his car keys. Three years down the line he was having fewer lucid episodes. When we could talk, he knew all about the dementia, that his days were numbered, despite the pharmaceutical research campaign I had raised from the garden of forking paths. One spring day we were on a mountainside in Montana, waiting for a chopper to pick us up after a picnic.

He said, "Ted – you know jack shit about SF, right?"

"Guilty as charged."

"So you never read any Sturgeon?"

I shook my head.

"Okay, do me a favour. Promise me you'll read *More than Human.*"

I recorded the name and said, "That's a promise. But why?"

"That book will explain to you what our little triumvirate really was. Soffy, me and you – we were three human beings with different talents combined into something

superhuman. Sturgeon had six, but we accomplished quite a bit working at half that strength."

That was one of the last times he could make sense when he talked. It was a blessing in a way, because he never knew about the pancreatic cancer that left Soffy's last ball of clay gathering dust. A year after that I attended Sigi's quiet funeral with my family. Unlike the other two members of the triumvirate, I have something to live for, with a loving wife and two good sons. I've still got my hair at sixty. I maintain my decoy job and suburban lifestyle. My neighbors are still banging on about the Singularity. SAVANT runs itself, for the money snowball is so big, it's self propelling.

I inherited the estates of Sigi and Sophocles. Not even Esmeralda knows she's married to the richest man in the world. I've been considering my options: sabotage the military-industrial complex; make China an offer she can't refuse; write a book; make a movie; start a new religion; turn Africa into a paradise; unify Ireland; finance interstellar exploration; restore individual privacy . . . The possibilities are endless, for I have turned out to be a singularity of sorts.

I am not quite sure what to do next.

But I shall think of something.

Tom Learmont is a Scot based in Johannesburg, South Africa, an editor and ghost writer. He has sold SF stories to Lavie Tidhar's World SF Blog, Singularities and Takamo Universe. He won The Sanlam Literary Award with a Swiftian afrofantasy called After the Eclipse. The firm Two Dogs published his Rogue Male -- sex and survival for the newly single man, which is now on Kindle in a version translated into "NewYorkese ".

Savant expresses his opinion that AI is being hyped to a ridiculous extent at present,and will always be a tool for Humankind , never a god.

Play it on Repeat

Brianna Suazo

Penny knew going to lunch with Leo was probably a bad idea. She really didn't have the time and preferred eating at her desk. Her boss's words kept bouncing around in her head. "Your argument is good, but it's too conventional," she had said. "You need to look at the case from every angle." Penny knew it was good criticism, useful, but it only made her feel more stuck.

To make matters worse, the sandwich place where she was meeting Leo was seven blocks from her firm. For the entire walk, she could feel the back of her pumps digging all the way through her tights and pulling away the top layer of ankle skin.

When she got there, he was loitering off to the side of the line, pressing his back against the list of artisanal cheeses. He didn't see her at first, he was staring at something in his hands. She angled herself so that he would spot her and waved.

He jumped, suddenly aware of her presence. "Hey, Penny!" he said with a small wave of his hand that hung stiffly at his side. He looked pretty much the same as she remembered, wearing a worn-out t-shirt, gray beanie, and dark jeans. He even had a slightly shorter version of his classic floppy, swept aside haircut.

They bought their sandwiches and sat at a table too close to the soda machine. He asked how she was doing. She gave him the short version; her move to the city after law school and how much she admired the partners at her firm. She started to talk about how she wanted to work on more domestic violence cases when she realized that, despite staring intently at her, he didn't seem to be listening all that closely.

Penny had that tight feeling in the back of her throat when she didn't know how to handle an awkward conversation.

"Are you still working in sound engineering?" she asked.

"Uh, no, not exactly. Well, sometimes. I'm mostly doing design stuff now, for like, video games and visualizations."

"Oh wow, that sounds really cool! Are you working for a studio or--?"

"No, no, mostly just freelancing."

"Oh, that's awesome. Have you done stuff for anyone I might've heard of?"

"Um, no, probably not."

The din of the voices around them rose up again to fill the silence. Penny was relieved to see Leo was almost done with his ham on rye. She ate her wrap faster, but not so fast he would notice.

"So, what are you doing in town?" she asked over the married couple debating the health of diet cola. "You said something in your text about visiting friends, but I don't really know who from Point Hugo lives out here."

"Oh, you know. Rick, Shelley, Fisher," he trailed off.

"Tyler Fisher? You guys get along now?"

"Oh, uh, yeah. We worked together at the diner out by I40 for a bit after I moved back, so we hang out."

"You worked at Pecans?" She couldn't help but laugh. "I'm surprised they even let you back in! We used to be complete little jerks there."

His face lit up into a grin. "God, yeah, remember when we tried to cheat the system on the unlimited pancakes?"

"Yes, and when they cut us off you stood up on the table and Rick started playing the Star-Spangled Banner on the harmonica?"

"It was beautiful!" he said.

"And your speech, what did you--?"

"Liberty and pancakes for all!" He put his fists in the air, the same show of victory he gave when the manager of Pecans had kicked them out so quickly, he forgot to give them the check. "God, don't you miss all that?"

"It was pretty fun," she said, "life was simpler back then." She got up to throw away her wrapper. He hastily got up, too. They walked out the side entrance by the patio, abandoned for winter. She glanced at her phone. 12:33. She had to get back.

"I knew it," Leo said, shaking his head with a small, satisfied smile. He suddenly pulled her close, toward the alley behind them. She could feel his hand brush through her hair. "I knew you were still in there."

"What? Leo I--"

Before she could get another word out, she suddenly felt dizzy and out of place. Leo's hand went back to his side, but she didn't feel it. Then suddenly they were back sitting in the sandwich shop. Everyone in the restaurant started moving backward, too fast to be real. She distantly felt herself stand up, but it was all wrong. She walked backward out the restaurant and moments later she was walking through the door of her office building and on the train and outside of her apartment and the whole time it was going faster and faster and faster with a faint whirring sound in the background like a VHS tape playing in jittery reverse. At some point, there was only colored light that might have been rooms or people blurring past her so quickly she felt sick and out of breath.

Then, just as it was getting so fast that Penny couldn't bear it, everything stopped moving. She was vaguely aware that she was laying on the ground and even more vaguely aware that someone--slowly coming into focus as Leo--was standing over her.

She thought for a moment that she had passed out on the sidewalk. But there was a ceiling above her. It was far away, metallic, and industrial. And there was this loud, crashing music that sounded like it was right next to her. She closed her eyes tight and opened them again. Leo looked different, too. His hair was longer and even floppier, he was dressed slightly differently than before, and he was skinnier. He kept looking down at her and then back at his hands with a big, goofy smile on his face that she couldn't even begin to comprehend.

She pushed herself up by her elbows and realized the floor was wet and sticky. There were people shuffling around her, endless legs and feet nearly stepping on her. The music was somehow getting louder. The tune even sounded familiar.

Leo bent down next to her, still grinning like an idiot. "Okay, Penny, listen to me and please don't freak out," he said, shouting over the crowd.

She knew how she knew the song. It was that band that Rick's cousin was in that they were obsessed with in high school. They practically had to beg them to come play in their town, in that dingy old warehouse that was owned by somebody's dad who wouldn't ask questions. The stage was barely visible from where she was sitting but it looked like them. She could have sworn they broke up back when--

"Pen, can you hear me?" Leo yelled again, interrupting her train of thought. He put his hand on her shoulder and she realized that the strands of her hair over it were dark blue.

"This can't be right," she finally said.

"So, uh, long story short," he said, "I can time travel."

Penny stumbled to her feet and immediately ran through the crowd away from him.

She could hear him calling behind her, but she kept running, pushing her way through the mass of people. Some of the faces that looked back at her were familiar; old classmates gave her looks that ranged from annoyed to concerned.

She raced into the warehouse's bathroom and clutched the sides of one of the dingy sinks, not sure if she was going to pass out or throw up. A startled, disheveled version of her sixteen-year-old self stared back at her with bloodshot eyes from across the mirror.

"Penny, are you in here?" a voice she recognized called from the door.

"Vera?" she called back in disbelief.

Her best friend stepped into the bathroom, and she still half-expected to see the tired mom who sent her Christmas cards every year. But no, it was bright-eyed, pink-streaked-haired Vera.

Without thinking, Penny just ran over and hugged her. All of this was still completely insane, but Vera would understand, they would figure it out together. The embrace caught Vera by surprise and the contents of her red cup sloshed onto Penny's arm.

"Oh, sorry, sorry," Vera said, grabbing paper towels from the barely-functional dispenser. "Leo said you got really claustrophobic and panicky all the sudden and I wanted to make sure you were okay."

Penny wrinkled her nose at the smell coming from her arm. "What were you drinking?"

"Rum and Coke," Vera said, dabbing her arm with the towels. "Sorry, hopefully the cops don't show up, 'cause frankly you're going to smell like a bar fight."

"Hey, is she okay?" Leo called in from the hallway.

"Yeah!" Vera called back. More quietly to Penny, she said, "he should probably drive you home. You look like you're going to be sick."

Penny nodded. "Yeah, tell him I'll be right out, okay?"

The moment Vera left, Penny climbed out through the window.

She hurried away from the warehouse. She could see the row of lights from the smattering of neighborhoods. She thought of going home, to her parents' house rather. But she couldn't bring herself to go that way. It would make it too real. Instead, she walked the other way with no particular destination in mind.

She found herself in front of Sunrise Creek. She sat down on the bank and let the water lap at her mud-caked combat boots. It was the same water she used to splash around in as a kid. A soft summer breeze rustled the trees. She hoped to make some sense of everything in the quiet, but all she found was a feeling settling in her chest that this was happening.

After a while, she felt a buzz in her pocket. She pulled out a chunky, black flip phone and opened it. After a bit of fumbling through menus, she found the new text.

'@Pecans. Plz come, Ill explain-L'

In front of her across the creek, there was an endless expanse of pitch-black farmland. She glanced back behind her, at the lights of the town. Then she looked left, where she could barely see the single glowing sign out by the highway. She sighed, stood up, and headed towards it.

She slid into the booth where he was waiting for her. "Take me back to the present."

"Hello to you, too," he said with a hint of amusement. "I got you a coffee."

"This isn't funny, Leo. I'm still trying to wrap my head around the fact that it's even possible, but I know it sure as hell isn't funny. Take me back, *now*."

He looked down at his shoes. "I…I can't."

"*What?*" she shouted. Several people turned to look at the two of them.

"Please, Penny, lower your voice," Leo whispered.

She ignored him and said even louder, "What do you mean, you can't?"

"I can only go backwards!"

She was on the verge of tears. "Why? Why the hell would you make me come back here?"

"We were happy here, Pen. Don't you remember?"

She let out a short, bitter laugh. "Yeah, being an angsty, pissed-off teenager in a tiny town was the highlight of my life."

"So, what," he said, suddenly accusatory, "you want to go back to being that bland, blazer-wearing lawyer?"

"*Excuse* me?"

"You used to be so interesting. God, you're the reason *I'm* interesting. What the hell happened?"

"Are you kidding me right now? Leo, I grew up!" she could feel her voice getting higher, a tell that she thought she had learned to control in law school. "I like my life. I worked my ass off for that life, and I make a difference."

Leo wrinkled his nose. "Filing contracts?"

She wanted to defend herself. She wanted to tell him the entire story of the time she won her first case, about the first client who sobbed in her arms, about the time a powerful attorney tried to intimidate her and failed. Or hell, the time she drove across the country by herself, the three times she had fallen in love, and how she still jammed to Knife Parade and Time Assassins on the train.

She bit her tongue, though. Leo didn't have any right to the person she was now. Instead, she just said, "get me out of here."

"I'm sorry, I should've asked first, I can't control it sometimes. You'll come around, I know you will," he said, softening his tone again and giving her that little half-smile that used to make her swoon. "This is the real you."

She felt like a trapped animal. She wanted to scrape at the walls of the diner, then at anything she could find in the woods outside, until she found some hole that would get her back home.

And then she found something. Not a hole, exactly, but a new angle.

"Did you know that Vera's father was an alcoholic?" she asked him.

He squinted at her, confused at this sudden turn in the conversation. "No, why?

She wasn't looking back at him. Instead, she took to examining the table and the coffee cup in front of her. Everything looked and felt perfect, especially the imperfection. There was a chip on the rim of one of the cups. She ran her thumb against it while she spoke. "Yeah, everyone thought Mr. Garrett was her dad, because he adopted her before they moved here. Her real dad died when she was little. She swore she'd never end up like him. She faked drinking at parties for years." Finally, she looked at him. A small, disbelieving smile crept across her face as the implications finally dawned on her. "You had *no idea*, did you, Leo?"

"Penny, what are you ta--"

"No, no, you shut up," she interrupted. "We're not in 2007, we're not even in Point Hugo! Time travel?" she scoffed. "God, you really tried to pass off that *thing* in there, casually holding a fucking rum and Coke in her hand, as my best friend. What, did you think I was going to go home to your creepy sims versions of my family and I wouldn't notice? How long did you think this was going to last?"

He was staring at her with wide eyes and she couldn't tell if the expression on his face was anger or fear.

"You were always so smart. I mean, obviously, this," she said while gesturing to everything around, "is incredible. I don't know how you did it and maybe once I would have cared. But Leo, for all your brilliance, you've always been so blind. You know why? Because you're so deeply, stupidly self-absorbed."

His hands balled into fists and she could hear that VHS whirring again, somewhere in the distance. Out of the corner of her eye, she saw a stool at the counter dissolve into nothing.

"What," she dug in further, "you couldn't build me, too? You seem to have no problem making creepy little puppets of everyone else."

Nothing disappeared this time, and she caught a shy half-smile on Leo's face. "You were too...I don't know. You were too alive."

His smile, along with the neon wall clock by the counter, disintegrated when he saw Penny's look of disgust.

"Penny, please. I'm sorry I lied, but you have no idea how hard I've worked on this. Stay here with me."

"No."

Her coffee cup dissolved too, and so did the man sitting two tables away.

"I love you," he said.

She was surprised when she felt a sudden pang of sadness. "No, you don't," she said softly, putting her hand over his. "You love your version of me."

The entire diner started to chip away, bit by bit, individual pixels flickered to black. And for a moment, they were both falling into nothingness. And with a jarring sudden jerk, she was back in the alley by the sandwich shop, face down on the concrete.

She was shaking and dizzy, and suddenly felt a sharp pain in the back of her head. Leo's hand was still on top of it. He was slumped against the building, eyes closed. She slowly lifted his hand up, pulling a long needle out of her head in the process. It hurt like hell; black spots formed in her vision as she pulled it out. There was a chip with circuitry taped to his hand, attached to another needle in the vein to his wrist. A series of wires, thicker than the one by the needle, went into his sleeve. With his head bent down, she could see that the wires led up his neck and disappeared into the back of his skull, lined up from ear to ear.

Penny still felt woozy, and it took a few seconds to look away from Leo's crumpled form. When she did, she realized three things at once. The first was that the time on her phone, now laying on the ground, read 12:35. The second, that a crowd was forming around them, including a woman wearing a nametag for the sandwich shop. She was on the phone, probably calling 911. Third, she realized that Leo wasn't breathing.

Brianna Suazo writes in Boulder, Colorado. She has been published in Spider Mirror Literary Journal, Havok, *and Toasted Cheese Literary Journal. In addition to writing, she enjoys exploring bookstores, hiking, and annoying her loved ones with inane trivia.*

The Man on the Pale Ass

Rev. Joe Kelly

When first he came, our caravan was a merry and a joyous band, men of many nations who swore by many names of God, united by a love of wonder, adventure, and the far-off places of the world. Rarely were ill words spoken; and never did any man come to blows.

He rode out of the setting sun one evening, as the songs rang the camp and lurid, exotic tales were told over the glimmering campfires. For the first time since starting my voyage in distant Kiev, I felt apprehension, as did many of my fellows, as we watched the shrunken figure's approach. Rare indeed is a lone traveler in the land of Turan, for the dangers are much and myriad in the wasted center of the world.

Gaunt beyond belief, his pale and scabby ass as sickly as he, our visitor greeted us with a rictus grin. I wondered what reason for mirth such a man should find, for clearly he had seen many deprivations: his body had been wasted unto the brink of death. And though I knew not yet the secret behind his cold and untwitching smile, still it made me shudder.

But we were not unkind hosts, and so we bade the man come and sit by our fire as he drew up. Unspeaking, his unsettling grin a frozen gash across his face, the man sat. He said not a word, and did no more to communicate with us other than to indicate with his hands his wish for food and drink. These we set before him; but our trepidation only increased, for he did not touch what was given him, but only sat and stared, and grinned his terrible grin.

Deeply disturbed, our mirthful talk and storytelling fell off; and swiftly we entered our cots that night, though few of us slept well, with our mysterious and grotesque visitor still sitting motionless, grinning at nothing.

The next day, the first man was found dead.

He had been drained of all his vital fluids, as one of the mummies that are occasionally found in the sands of Araby and Altishahr, unearthed from their sleep of centuries by the shifting winds. The previous night, he had been as healthy and mirthful as any of us; now, the waste of aeons had seeped deep within his flesh, and his sinews crumbled at our touch. Those who found him cried out in horror, and wailed with the heartache of a beloved friend; but it was not long before they all turned to shouting, to angry accusations of diabolic murder. And the subject of their shouting, as may easily be guessed, was our mysterious visitor.

He was accused of sorcery, of demonism, and the terrible evidence lain against him was difficult to refute. And the man who had ridden in on the pale ass did not try to defend himself, or plead for his life. He merely sat, as he had the last night, and smiled up at us, with that terrible grin that showed his hideously yellowed teeth, the gums retracted almost to to bone. The silent grin only stoked our terror and our anger further, and we shouted all the more at him, as fearful beasts before a predator; and we received no more answer than we would have from the stalking lion.

Having offered no defense, but merely remained silent in the face of our accusations, he thereby condemned himself; and he was summarily hacked to pieces. And we all blanched and swung our blades all the harder when we saw the blood that ran from him was not healthy bright-red, but viscous, dark, and ichorous, with a foul smell that told of some monstrous unknown ailment. His animal was driven off as a poxy beast, and the remains were left to dry out beneath the hammering sun, forgotten upon those illimitable plains of Asia.

By the following evening, the incident was already half-forgotten; the sorcerer on the pale ass was dead, and the friends of the slain man were given space to mourn. The rest of us had just begun to regain our former merriment. And then, the cry went up: "The man! The man on the pale ass!"

We started up as one in horror, and looked out across the plain. And there he was: riding into our camp, just as he had the night before, swaying upon his half-dead animal, grinning his awful grin.

At once an arrow was sped that struck him full in the chest. He fell dead at once, and the animal began to run; but this time it was spared no mercy, and further arrows feathered the beast until at last it collapsed and fell dead as well. We cringed at that sight, for the pale ass made no more sound than did its master.

There was no more merriment that night. Prayers were muttered over the fires; and men looked askance at once another, wondering what it could all mean.

The next morning, another man was found dead, in the same ghastly manner as the first, and there was much fury and wailing in the camp. No connection could be found between the two: the first had been a young man, a servant, one of the Turanian Turks who made up the bulk of the caravan band. The second was an elderly Druze scholar, the sole representative of his people among our band, and a man towards whom none felt ill will. Indeed, he and the servant boy alike were well-liked among the caravan, and neither had given any man of that band any meaning for animosity.

But, with such a curse that now seemed to follow us, reasons were swiftly invented; and men were no longer able to look at each other as brother travelers.

That evening, the man on the pale ass returned yet again.

A furious panic swept the camp at his appearance. As a horde we descended upon him at once and hacked both him and his beast to pieces. This time, no chances were taken. The remains were burned, and many a prayer was said over the ashes. The Mahomedans, the Jews, my fellow Christians, all besought God in our own ways to free us of this terrible curse, and to ensure that the demon who rode the pale ass did not return to haunt us further. Among us was a Mongol shaman, an exceeding rarity in that age; and, though to an outsider it might seem a blasphemy, even his ancient heathen rites were sought as further protection, so desperate were we to be free of this curse.

But it was all for naught. The next day, a third man was found dead, a brittle, crumbling corpse, as though the desert itself had drained him both of life and time. And this time, there was no wailing, but much glaring and muttering.

When the man on the pale ass inevitably returned the following evening, it was the spark that ignited our powderkeg. Men swiftly fell to shouting, to blaming one another for the terrible scourge that dogged us. What was once a loving brotherhood split along old wounds; the Mahomedans gathered together, and they accused the rest of us of having brought this dread affliction to the caravan. The Christians shouted back, declared that their faith was pure; it must have been one of the Mahomedans--or one of the Jews. And the Jews, rather than shrink before the accusation, stood in a small phalanx, their swords held in tight grips, and railed against the rest of us, dared us to try to do to armed fighting men what countless pogroms had done to women and old men and children.

I myself remained fearfully silent; for I could see already it was useless. Even if there were some accursed member of our band, they would never be found out in time. And, I feared, it was exactly this that the mysterious visitor wanted; for, while we shouted and threw baseless accusations at each other, the man who rode the pale ass merely sat, and watched silently; and it seemed to me his demoniac grin only grew.

At last, it was decided by an uneasy consensus that the shaman must be responsible. At first, he tried to defend himself; but we were in no mood to listen to reason. And there were none to speak for him, save for an elderly imam who had begged from the beginning for all to cease the terrible accusations, to unite once more and to pray for deliverance. But we were long past prayer.

At the last, as he was tied up and laid before the grinning man, the shaman cursed us: "This will not stop with my murder! You all know it to be true! You will all join me in death--it comes for us all!"

The mob would listen to no more; a qama was plunged into his chest, and he was left dead before the grinning man. And with that, the caravan withdrew, and watched for some sign from our baleful visitor; but he gave none. A hideous tableau it was, an image out of barbarous antiquity, a fearful tribe sacrificing its beloved to appease the capricious whims of a monstrous dark god.

And I was not alone in noting the horror of the scene; for I saw, while the others watched the grinning man, the Jews, sensing the coming horrors with the sixth sense of a people long persecuted, had gathered up in secret and now withdrew from the caravan. A desperate people they were, for to leave the caravan trails in that merciless land is to court death; but, they must have thought, better to risk being lost and stranded atop the terrible steppe of Turan than to stay among a people whose blades will surely be turned upon you soon. Would that my fellow Christians had chosen the same course; for what was soon to come may be easily guessed.

The next dawn found another wasted corpse, and the absence of the Jews was at last noted. Curses of good riddance were spat upon their trail, and, without bothering to bury the bodies, we packed up in silence and resumed our journey, my fellow Christians riding somewhat apart from the others and exchanging dark looks with our former brothers. And this time, the man on the pale ass rode with us openly.

There was another confrontation that evening. This time, only we Christians were left to be blamed. With none others left to deflect to, we found ourselves surrounded by a furious mob; and in spite of the pleadings of the wise old imam, only one outcome could possibly come of it. I know not who drew their blade first; but at once the camp was a furious melee, shamshirs and tulwars singing, whipping arced droplets of blood, as brother fell upon brother and we hacked each other to screaming sanguine gore.

All the Christians were slaughtered. All, save myself, who, knowing nothing whatever of the art of mortal combat, hid in terror, thinking to escape amid the bodies. But I was swiftly found, and would have been put to death, were it not for the imam, who threw himself over by body, crying, "Enough! This must end! This man's life I claim in the name of God, the Almighty, the Magnificent."

The imam's wishes were begrudgingly granted; I was not killed. But I was thrown out of the caravan, and left to walk the brutal desert plains of Turan, carrying nothing but enough food and water to make it back on foot to the nearest caravansary.

I was broken by this turn. All my worldly possessions had been tied up in the caravan; now, I had nothing but the clothes on my back, which turned to rags as I wandered the plains of Turan, a beggar and a drifter. Moon after moon of mendicant misery did I spend in that desolate land, from which all the romance I had invested it with was swiftly drained. I found myself trapped in the ugly underbelly of Turan, the desperate, scratching fight for survival which breeds men little better than animals. And an animal I became, a rotten-mouthed parasite who would dance a miserable dance for a morsel of meat, who would grovel and debase himself for a drop of wine; and, on occasion, who would murder for a pinch of silver, or a chunk of moldy flatbread to stave off starvation for another day.

It was a full year of my life that I spent in that condition, before, wandering amid a band of fellow beggar-pilgrims, I came upon a face I recognized. It was one of my former companions from the caravan, a Turkish Mahomedan. Being reduced to the same state of misery, we felt no ill will towards one another for the terrible slaughter that had separated us. It had been a state of madness, a fever that had never really broken, but had merely abated to a slow burning despair.

That night, he told me of the ultimate fate of the caravan; and here, I record his testament for posterity:

"Of course it did not end with the slaughter of the Franks. You may be thankful, at the very least, that you did not have to witness what came next; for the anger and the fear and the cruelties only multiplied. The man on the pale ass did not leave us, as we had prayed he would after we were rid of all the dhimmi. No, indeed, we continued to find dead men, night after night, drained of all their vitals.

"Inevitably, we turned upon ourselves. Arab turned upon Persian, Turk upon Hindi; sect turned against sect, clan against clan. For fully three days we sat in one broken camp, and raided one another, seeking out the one who had brought the malediction against us. Mad as we were, we did not yet split apart, so fearful that the curse would follow us on, and so we sought desperately to slay its source.

"Of course, it did no good. No man among that number had ever brought curse against the rest. We should have guessed as much. What reason was there ever for it? Why should any man bring a curse that killed indiscriminately?

"It was only when the old imam was found dead that, somehow, we were able to recognize the truth. In sheer terror we broke our camp and fled in all directions, blindly rushing across the steppe. Mad we were, for we risked the same fate that the man on the pale ass brought to us; but we were as fear-crazed hares, heedless of what lay ahead.

"Even this did not save us. And why should it have? The man and his ass had returned from the dead more than once. It was only mortal terror that gave us any hope. I had followed a larger band of my fellows, and we were at last a day away from a caravansary we knew well, when, that evening, a cry went up. The man on the pale ass was approaching us. I, at last, gave up all hope, and fell prostrate with a cry of despair; but the others grabbed what they could and fled screaming into the desert. The man on the pale ass merely changed his course, and followed one of them.

"Thus it continued. I made my way to Samarqand, and there met with a few fellow survivors of the caravan. The man had dogged each of their bands, relentless in his course of destruction. Even the walls of Samarqand were no sanctuary, for they said another survivor had recently been found dead in the same manner.

"In pairs and small bands we have wandered Turan ever since, a self-pariah folk, seeking some respite from the curse, praying at all manner of shrines, even to those heathen idols to Buddha and the older, stranger gods which dot these lands. No good did it do us: though the man on the pale ass has taken his time of late, still he dogs our trails. I hear, from time to time, tales from the last few pairs and bands of survivors, that they will still find the man approaching their evening quarters; and that, the following morning, another one of our former brothers is dead, and the man on the pale ass is already riding off, in search of his next victim, in accordance with some inscrutable plan of his.

"I have heard fewer and fewer of these tales; and of late, they have ceased to reach me at all. I fear, my friend, that we are the last; and, I think, you will be the last to know of this tale. For I can feel his approach, like a hot and fetid wind across the desert. I know he comes for me next. And you, I think, shall be his last."

My brother of the caravan was not wrong. That very evening, the man on the pale ass rode into the beggar camp and sat at our fire, grinning at us both. And the next morning, my erstwhile friend was dead; and all the other beggars cried out in fear, and spat upon the ground next to us and made signs to ward off curses and the evil eye. But we heeded them not. I, and the grinning man, we looked only at each other; he, fixed in his hideous and unchanging mirth; I, in a state of resignation.

But, much to my consternation, I lived to see the next day, and the next.

The man on the pale ass did not leave my side. He followed me everywhere; and as I left the beggar caravan and sought a nearby caravansary, he followed me still. At last, somehow, it came to me what he wanted: he wished for me to record all this. I have spent my last fals on writing implements, and I record this story, knowing that I shall not live to see the following morning. It is a dread prospect, to at last learn how it feels to be killed in so ghastly a fashion. But I am at peace with this; even though I should undergo the torments of hell at the hands of the man on the pale ass, still I am yet at peace, for life is a never-ending torture of starvation and the grinding dull misery of mendicancy, and above all the hovering cloud of fear that has followed me since that fateful journey with the caravan. Death, I think, shall be a sweet release; for God will judge a good

Christian rightly, and I shall not be forced to endure any more past this last night.

Post-script:

It was with no little shock that I awoke this morning, not only to find myself alive, but to find that the man on the pale ass is, at last, gone. I can only assume that he wished for his tale to be told, that he followed me at the last to ensure I would tell of it, and then departed.

It seems a mad thing at first, that such an inscrutable demon as he, whose motives I still do not understand in the slightest, should follow the same tactics as a petty bandit, and leave a sole survivor to spread the terror of his tale. But, then, I suppose the man on the pale ass was not quite as inscrutable as I had supposed. He found endless mirth in the awful acts which he performed, after all; and, as vain and arrogant as any mighty mortal, he demanded his tale be told, that his legend be spread far and wide.

I have obliged him, then. And I will not burn this manuscript, as I am tempted to do; for to do so, I suspect, will call his wrath down upon me. I shall tell his tale, as he wished. And, maybe, he will be lucky, and the sole man who lives to tell his tale will not be dismissed as a desert-crazed beggar--if only I might find a scholar, equally as mad as myself, who is willing to listen.

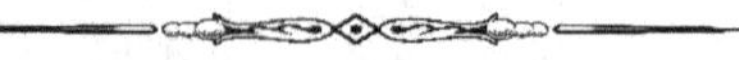

Rev. Joe Kelly is a connoisseur of cheap beer, good metal, and quality fantasy. He has been published in Cirsova and Heroic Fantasy Quarterly. He can be occasionally contacted on twitter at @reverendjoefake when he bothers to check it.

Our werewolf anthology **Call of the Wyld** is now out in hardback, with a brand new cover and larger, eyesight-friendly pages. It's still available as a paperback or ebook, too. Twelve grisly tales of fur and fury:

Werewolves on the prowl!
Werewolves at your door!
Werewolves in space!
Werewolves in your nightmares!

All new stories of the night, when the moon is full and the blood drips crimson dark. Tales of loss, hope, adventure and revenge. Wild and weird stories of feasting, stalking, hunting and abandon. Read them in daylight—and lock your doors tight.

Order now at www.wyldblood.com/books

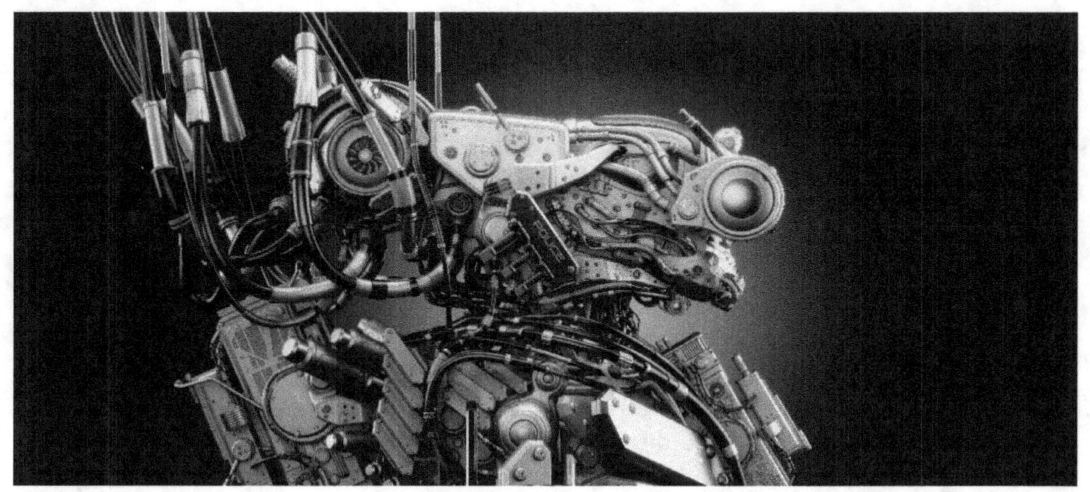

Testing Dash Nine

Mark Rigney

The second part of *Taming Dash Nine* – first part in Wyldblood #4

I realize I've mentioned this before, but the honest truth deserves repeating: I'm a freedom fighter, not a terrorist. And that goes for everyone here in the Nest, and really everyone on our side of the Free Appalachian border. Would the proud, stubborn, bull-headed people of the New Confederation agree with my assessment? Probably not.

Need I also mention that having reached the venerable age of twenty-two, I do not appreciate other people telling me how to do my job, and that includes the Nest's ranking officer, Lieutenant Jalen Kelsey, my long-time mentor. I'd always held him in the highest regard, but lately, I'd begun to see myself as his tactical equal. The child is father to the man, and all that that entails. Or so I liked to hope.

But on that particular afternoon, I was not his equal. I had been summarily summoned to the lieutenant's windowless office, a full six stories below ground, and the lieutenant and I faced off from opposite sides of his all-metal desk, a barely refurbished, two-ton relic dating from approximately World War II.

I cleared my throat. "Sir? Am I in trouble?"

The lieutenant drew a long breath through his nose, which made him sound like old ductwork in need of a good scrubbing. "Remind me, Corporal, of your course-work background."

I'd been sitting on my hands for several minutes (I had a notion that this would keep me from outright screaming), but the lieutenant's question was so unexpected that I wound up rocking back and forth on my palms. I must have looked like a squirming toddler, caught mere seconds before in the act of picking her nose.

"Sir," I said, "relevant coursework would include five years of field ops, eight years of programming, re-programming, and related applied computer studies, along with extended intensives in weaponry, explosives, wilderness survival, urban survival, orienteering, field medicine, counterfeiting, basic engineering, relevant math, the chemistry of poisons, and an eight-year immersive focus in classic, pre-pandemic literature."

At this, Lieutenant Kelsey gave his cuticles a tired stare. "Corporal Robin Dell, budding Shakespearean scholar and occasional field operative. Doesn't exactly sound like a lethal cocktail, does it?"

"Sir, I object to the inference that I am now some sort of threat."

"You had a very straightforward mission. Not a simple one, no, but clear-cut. Precise."

"Sir, the files we brought back, the hard drives—that's the kind of intel that could crack the entire New Confederation!"

Lieutenant Kelsey rose from his chair and slapped one palm, hard, on the reverberating metal desktop. "Yes!" he cried. "We could crack every New Confed password and be heroes, at least for our side. Or, we could be dead in ten minutes, because instead of sticking to your assignment, you also brought home a fully functional Centaur Seven! A Centaur Seven that is, I hope, I *pray*, still standing in our best loading bay, but could at any moment shoot its way down here and wipe out every living being in this entire complex."

I sat as far back as my chair would allow, eyes wide and my mouth clamped shut. I wanted to say that Dash Nine would never hurt a fly, not now, not after I'd re-set his protocols—or, to be fair, after I'd *accidentally* re-set his protocols, using nothing more than a random Shakespeare quote. Crazy, I know, but it's true: a single, impulsively muttered dose of the Bard had rendered security bot Centaur Seven Dash Nine Sixty-Five not just harmless, but amicable.

Dash Nine, of course, swore that he was now mine to command. But who, besides me, had any reason to believe?

Slowly, as if driven downward by exhausted hydraulics, the lieutenant eased himself back into his seat. He rubbed his face with both hands, and reached for the smallest of the several monitor screens on his desk, adjusting it so I could see. The display showed security camera footage, a live feed of Loading Bay One, in which Dash Nine stood patiently by the same cargo van we'd arrived home in three days before. The bot stood so still that he might as well have been a statue, and I took this as further evidence of Dash's perfect fealty. I'd ordered him to stay put and wait for me, and that was exactly what he was doing. I'd also ordered him to avoid scanning local data networks, or to use his exceptional sensory apparatus to learn more about his surroundings. To this, too, he'd acquiesced, saying, in his warm, pleasant baritone, "Of course, Robin. After all, 'Curiosity killed the cat.'"

But had Dash Nine actually refrained from plugging in, or surfing the Nest's constantly scrambled but ultimately vulnerable hot spots? There was simply no way to tell.

The lieutenant let out another prodigious, through-the-nose sigh. A man with paler skin would likely have shown his exasperation through a pink-red flush, but Lieutenant Kelsey came from darker stock. In the right light, I thought he actually looked a lot like my father—or what I could remember of him.

"Robin," he said at last, "we can't let that thing come down here, and because it knows our location, we can't let it out. Your decision to adopt this walking hunk of hardware leaves me two options, so far as I can see. One is to do our best to destroy it, which would be risky, since I assume it comes with its share of self-preservation directives. The other is to bury it right where it is. Seal up the room, pull every possible data port, and line the walls with lead—lead we don't have, by the way."

An image from Poe's "Cask of Amontillado" flickered through what passes, in my head, for a memory bank. There stood Montressor, his brick-work mounting higher, while Dash Nine, doomed and imprisoned, took the place of Fortunado. Would Dash, like Fortunado, cry out, "For the love of God!"? That would be a tragedy on multiple levels, but I could see the lieutenant's perspective. Letting Dash Nine go was suicide. Sure, at present we were scrambling Dash's feeds to the point where he couldn't transmit so much as a pixel, much less his location, back to his former New Confed handlers, but if he got out? Once he was a block away, he'd be able to network freely, after which he'd be spotted and re-acquired. The Nest would be fatally compromised.

Unless, of course, I was in the right, and Dash Nine was now our greatest ally and asset.

Still staring at the screen with sad, marmoreal concentration, the lieutenant said, "If you can find a way to convince me that it's really on our side, wonderful. I'll give you three hours."

"Robin!" said Dash Nine, as I stepped into Loading Bay One. "I was wondering when you'd make your entrance."

Pleased, I attempted a little red-carpet sashay, but since flirtatious elegance was a facet of life with which I had no direct experience, I suspect I came off looking like a stork tripping over its own feet.

As I regained my balance, the facts of my new friend reasserted themselves with ugly force. Centaur Sevens exist to do two things: patrol, and kill. And what on earth would stop Dash Nine, if he chose, from spattering my guts all over the echoing, white-painted, brick walls? Let's face it, he was the size of a horse, complete with four muscular, hydraulic legs and an armored torso that sprouted from approximately where an equine neck should have begun. Squared-off shoulders gave way to stocky arms that terminated in cunning metal fingers. The head at the top lacked all features, and it looked remarkably like the casing of an old outboard motor. His sleek paneling, from tip to absent tail, had been rendered in various tones of black and gray, and while here and there he showed nicks and abrasions, signs that he'd seen combat more than once, in the main, he was so dapper and polished that he looked ready for a black-and-white ball.

"Dash," I said, "have you been doing what I told you?"

"You asked me to remain here. I have remained. You asked me not to access networks of any kind, and I have refrained from doing so. You did not specifically abjure me from studying my surroundings, so you will permit me to say that the drab, dreary, high-ceilinged and inherently lonely space in which we stand is an affront to the soul, a place devoid of spirit and incapable of inspiration. It reeks of motor oil, grease, and corroded rubber. Also, one of the gray-water pipes crossing the ceiling in the northwest corner is beginning to leak. I estimate that the leak will become apparent to the human eye in approximately nine hours and twenty-seven minutes."

The smile on my face slid toward the goofy, I-can't-help-it variety. Every word that Dash Nine spoke left me feeling unreasonably happy, strangely warm, girlishly shy. Despite having spent most of my life teasing others about their fake, play-acted bot-crushes, I'd never had the least scrap of faith that such a thing could actually happen, especially to me. My rapid conversion felt like a delightfully painless comeuppance.

"Never mind about the pipes," I said. "We have a problem."

Dash Nine nodded his planar head with something approaching clerical solemnity. "We are locked on the horns of a dilemma. Specifically, we have come face to face with the Leinster Conundrum."

Leave it to a robot to conjure up a term I'd never so much as heard of. "What," I demanded, "is a Leinster?"

"Murray Leinster, *homo sapiens*, male, born Will F. Jenkins, science fiction writer of the twentieth century. His short story 'First Contact' details a deep space encounter between humans and an alien race in which neither group dares to leave, lest their home world be threatened by the other faction, representing as they must a potentially hostile and newly encountered species. An impasse occurs—"

"—and that impasse is the Leinster Conundrum."

Sounding bashful, Dash Nine said, "I have just now coined the term."

This brought me up short. Was Dash Nine serious that he'd just invented and defined a concept all on his own? Centaur Seven units were exceptional—phenomenal, even, being simultaneously the best and most dangerous bot the New Confederation had ever dreamed up—but they flat out weren't capable of inferences or analogies, much less inventing new names for other people's ethical quandaries.

"Right," I said. "So, how did this Leinster guy solve the problem?"

"The two races swapped spacecraft, then used each other's ships to get home. This provided a viable détente. Unfortunately, our situation is not sufficiently analogous. I am mobile, and your Nest is not. We cannot swap crews."

"So, the Leinster Conundrum ultimately doesn't apply."

Dash Nine did his best to look chastened. He hung his head, then twisted his clasped fingers, for all the world like some fretful parent, worrying over missing children.

"Right," I said. "Here's what we're going to do. You're going to temporarily disarm."

"I am?"

Turning, I stared up at the ceiling, into the high corners where I knew multiple half-hidden cameras were currently observing my every twitch. "Hey!" I said. "As a show of faith, the centaur is going to disarm itself. And when it's done, send some people in besides just me. Trust is a two-way street, yeah?"

I didn't expect a reply, and I didn't get one. With my attention back on Dash Nine, I said, "You can disarm by yourself, right?"

"That is a complicated question. But in the main, yes. I shall commence."

Several of Dash Nine's body panels slid up and back, a nerve-wracking sight, since this meant it was now set to unleash a hailstorm of bullets and other projectiles, most likely toward me. Sure enough, the muzzles of various guns and other weaponry poked into view, so many that Dash began to resemble a massive robotic hedgehog. I spotted a grenade launcher, a flame thrower, and several other tube-like appendages that I couldn't immediately identify.

"Stand clear," Dash said, and as I shuffled hurriedly backward, all manner of bullets, shell-casings, and other oddments began popping out from the centaur's body, pinging around, and crash-landing like scattered dice on the cement floor. On Dash's opposite side, the spray of ammunition banged and rattled off the sides of the adjacent cargo van, which Dash Nine, ever obedient, had not yet stepped away from. The racket was tremendous, and the sheer volume of projectiles that bot ejected? Jaw-dropping.

Just like that, it was over. A final bullet popped free, arced through the air, and landed with a metallic *clink* on the floor.

Dash Nine looked around with what, in a human, would have been a rueful expression. "Messy, isn't it?"

That pulled a belly laugh from me, which frankly felt wonderful. It also gave me an idea. "Hey, Dash," I said. "We're gonna do a thing. In a minute. But I've gotta ask, first. What you just did took care of all the mechanical ordnance, but what about fuel for the flame thrower? Or electrical for the taser?"

"Certain fluids will need to be drained. This requires assistance. In terms of power supply, the only way to truly disarm a Centaur Seven is to let its battery run down."

I'd thought as much. "Are there any liquids you can release on your own, on command? Something harmless, something we can easily refill again, after?"

"Of course. What did you have in mind?"

Grinning, I stepped forward to whisper in what I supposed might be Dash Nine's ear. "I have a work-around for the Leinster Conundrum. Here's the plan…"

Not twenty minutes later, Dash Nine's disarmament display had paid its first dividends. Lured in equal parts by Dash's act of good faith and their own innate curiosity, reps from nearly all of the Nest's many departments had assembled to examine their mortal enemy up close, led by Lieutenant Kelsey. There was a great deal of muttered hemming and hawing, but after several long minutes, not one of my understandably indoctrinated brothers-in-arms had thought to address Dash directly. I all but rolled my eyes. It was like being at a party where the exact wrong mix of guests has assembled, each one more skittish and awkward than the next, making it impossible to relax and socialize.

But right on cue, and without warning, Dash Nine let loose a stream of water-based coolant from the nebulous space between his hind legs, and that liquid rained down, spattering the floor, and leaving my robot friend looking exactly like a horse taking a long, unselfconscious piss.

My Nest-buds gaped. And then, as the jet of coolant slackened to a final dribble, they did exactly what Dash Nine and I had hoped they would: they burst into guffaws of hysterical laughter.

Murray Leinster had it right, as I learned later by perusing his work in the Nest's fiction database. When building trust, there's no better bedrock than shared laughter.

Trustworthy or not, the lieutenant and I agreed that actions in the field ultimately mattered more than the comedy of fake urine, and so, two days later, I found myself trudging uphill in a Brown County ravine, the sort of scenic oak and maple forest that even the New Confederation had had the good sense to keep open for hiking trails and family fun. Normally, I'd have had a human field op as my second, probably Liam James, but instead, it was Dash Nine who clanked along beside me. We had dead brown leaves underfoot, and a canopy of varied green above. I'm sure it would have been a gorgeous day for a long, woodsy tramp, except for two facts: it was pouring cats and dogs, and the combined radio and cell tower at the top of the ridge came with a complement of two New Confed monitors, possibly well-armed.

True, it was also possible that the station monitors were klutzy, acne-riddled interns not even done with what passed, north of the border, for college, but in my line of work? Assuming the worst is the master key to survival.

"Dash," I said, as the raindrops pelted my face and soaked my woodland camo, "I know we banked on rain, but this is ridiculous."

"Updated radar suggests we are operating directly beneath a strengthening supercell. Optimal conditions for excess precipitation will continue for at least another twenty-four minutes."

"Wonderful."

We'd wanted rain—built the day around it, in fact—but this was fast becoming absurd. I could all but see the leaves on the slope above slithering downhill, sliding one over the next like so many surfers at a crowded beach.

Unperturbed, Dash Nine took the opportunity to announce that the quality of mercy is not strained, that it droppeth like a gentle rain from Heaven, to which I said, in disbelief, "You call this a *gentle* rain?"

Still trudging, hooves slipping back a foot for every yard gained, Dash Nine said, "'The rain, it raineth every day.'"

I harrumphed. "That's a lie."

"'Much rain wears the marble.'"

"Okay, are we done now?"

"'When shall we three meet again? In thunder, lightning, or in rain?'"

With expert timing, lightning flickered overhead, followed a split second later by a burgeoning moan of thunder, a rising cascade of quarry-like detonations that made me think of Rip Van Winkle playing nine-pins in the Catskills. That was a range of peaks I supposed I'd never see, even though they were protected by the Colonial Corridor, a semi-stable alliance of ex-states that featured a government even more permissive and progressive than my own. A lot of New Confederation territory lay between here and there, none of it friendly to me.

Slogging along, battling the mud below and the rain above, we fought our way uphill, and with every hard-won step, we breathed in the scent of wood-rot, that heady, fecund odor that rises from every downed log in this part of the world on all but the coldest winter days. Twenty yards to go, then ten, and at last we'd clambered up the hollow's final slope to emerge on the twin dirt tracks of a narrow, puddled service road that led, some fifty feet to our right, to a frighteningly lofty antennae tower, its strong, graceful geometry jutting skyward like the prow of some celestial ship, up and up, until it lost itself in an Oort cloud of gray, tumbling raindrops. At its base stood our target, a cinderblock hut no more than fifteen feet on a side, and looking entirely unworthy to be worshipping at the feet of such a magnificent construct.

There wasn't a vehicle to be seen, just as we'd hoped for and expected, and the weedy road dead-ended, as if too exhausted to go farther, at the hut's front door.

Were we in plain sight of any satellites, drones, or other camera systems? The former two, working presumably from above, would be blinded by the low clouds—again, we'd chosen this day and this particular low pressure system intentionally—and the downpour would also blind whatever security cams had been mounted on the building. Thanks to the sluicing rain, and even knowing full well what objects I was facing, they were hard to make out. Given my tactical gear, I had to assume that I looked, to anyone watching, like a smudgy tree or perhaps a shrub. Dash Nine, blanketed in camouflage netting, would look much the same.

The time was eight thirty-seven in the morning, seven minutes later than we'd expected to arrive. So it goes with field ops. Sometimes, you get in and out like well-calibrated clockwork. Other days, it rains like an end-of-days plague, and when it does, even the best of well-planned timetables slips uncontrollably through your fingers.

As if reading my mind, Dash Nine pulled up Robbie Burns, delivered in a quite passable Scots brogue. "'The best laid schemes,'" he whispered, sounding amused, "'gang aft a'gley.'"

"Scan for me," I said. "And next time you hit that quote, don't leave out the mice."

"You have a soft spot for rodents?"

"I have a soft spot for the underdog. Now, is anybody home in there, or did they head out for coffee the way they're supposed to?"

If it hadn't been pouring, I might have overheard a whirring buzz from deep inside Dash Nine's chest, but instead, my eardrums were overwhelmed by some nameless rain-god's fury, punctuated now and then by distant blows from Thor's noisy hammer.

After a moment, Dash said, "Pardon the delay. Passwords and protocols were updated two days ago. A hack was required."

"And?"

"The compound contains no human occupants. It follows that the standard complement of station monitors has followed their morning routine."

"Any non-human living occupants?"

I was thinking of guard dogs, so I was surprised when Dash Nine said, "There is a hamster. I believe it is caged."

"Oh, thank God for that. Wouldn't want to be gunned down by a feral hamster."

"Very sensible," said Dash Nine, agreeably. "Such a desire, in your species, would be a sign of impending madness."

I smirked, and rain wandered into my mouth at the upraised corner. "What do you think? Did the New Confeds update their passwords because you went missing?"

A fresh blitz of lightning, followed by an immediate thunder clap, nearly drowned out Dash Nine as he said, "Speculation is the hobgoblin of little minds."

There he went, inventing again. Freestyling instead of quoting. Impending signs of robotic madness?

"Come on," I said. "Let's get this over with."

"As discussed, I am jamming their security feeds as of…now."

My smile went so wide, it was threatening to split my face. Who needed Liam James, or any other human sidekick? I had a freaking Centaur Seven.

With my pistol drawn, we marched as one toward the door. Dash Nine's threat assessment was surely accurate, but not worth losing my life over. Maybe, somehow, there was still someone inside, and maybe that someone had a ready, loaded gun. I'm a

freedom fighter, yes, and never a terrorist—and Lieutenant Kelsey is correct, this isn't a hot war, it's a war of destabilizing infiltration, courtesy of yours truly and a thousand more like me—but labels don't matter when it's kill or be killed.

"Relax," said Dash Nine, traipsing along beside me. "The hamster is unarmed."

"Very funny. Gimme some room."

But, of course, the door was locked, and so my heroic entrance fizzled like a firecracker suddenly dunked in the Wabash.

Dash Nine said, "Ah. A recalcitrant door knob. The finest in state-of-the-art security."

"Oh, put a sock in it."

My centaur cocked his head in what I took to be a critical stare as I knelt, holstered my weapon, and withdrew the lock-picking kit that is an essential component of my utility belt. Locks, as even Liam will admit, are a specialty of mine. In the main, he's the one with the clever hands, a talent he demonstrates almost daily on the Nest's junker piano, a scavenged upright on which he can play virtually anything: Chopin and Gershwin, Professor Longhair and Tardyboy Joe. Or at least, he could, in past days—before Dash Nine tased him, on my order (and for the best of good reasons), during our last foray across enemy lines. Would Liam and his newly clumsy fingers be able to fight back to his previous level of proficiency? I hoped so. It would wreck him forever if he couldn't play.

After shoving these thoughts into the mud beneath my boots, I got a firm grip on my favorite tension bar and bore down on the business at hand, entirely confident in the outcome. A lock like this wouldn't take me thirty seconds—or so I thought.

Several minutes later, Dash Nine leaned in, dripping rainwater, and said, "I could take a turn, if you like."

"No, I got it."

"I will remind you that, on arrival, we were already seven minutes behind schedule."

"Noted, thanks."

"The coffee shop to which the station monitors typically repair is only five minutes away by car, truck, or other wheeled conveyance. If ordering time can be averaged out to ten minutes, and assuming that they left on time at eight twenty-five, as is their usual habit, then we have approximately six minutes remaining to finish our business and be gone."

Stupid lock. I reached for a more delicate, slimmer tension bar, but kept the same pick. In seconds, I had four of the five pins sitting on the lock mechanism's shear line, but the fifth and final one simply would not go.

Leaning close, Dash Nine sighed as if humanity had long since broken his metal heart. "Robin Dell, even if the rain slows the progress of the coffee-addicted guards by one minute each way, our margins for error are becoming increasingly untenable."

"Fine," I said, and I jerked my tools free and rocketed to my feet. "You do it."

From the smallest finger of his left hand, Dash Nine smoothly extended a winsome combo tool that surely belonged in every Swiss army knife, and in two seconds flat, the lock was picked.

In a sulky voice that I tried to deep-six but couldn't, I said, "You've still got their security feeds fritzed?"

"'A thousand times, yes.'"

Liam, for what it's worth, would have simply said, "Affirmative."

"On three," I said, one hand clutching my pistol, the other on the door knob. My pulse was hammering so hard, I could feel it in my jaw. "One…two…three!"

We blew through the door like two cops on a drug bust, and it's a good thing we did, too, because while the room was mostly what we'd expected—a work station with a desktop, a sofa, a cot, various shelves, a tall metal storage cabinet, two sturdy CPUs, and, yes, a hamster squatting in a ten-gallon tank and nibbling sunflower seeds—there was also a Semblance-4, and it rose as we charged in, pulled a revolver from its belt, and got a bead on my startled face.

I hurled myself to the left, firing as I did so. Did I mention I'm a crack shot? I am. But not necessarily when leaping sideways and being more or less run over from behind by a protective Centaur Seven. What exactly happened I may never know, but the next two seconds were shockingly, bracingly loud as multiple weapons went off at close range in that tight, bunker-like space, and the Semblance-4's neck snapped backward as a bullet (mine, I think) caught it right in its perfect forehead. Half an instant later, its whole body flew backward into the wall, courtesy of multiple shots from Dash Nine, and when it slithered to the floor, tendrils of twining smoke rose from half a dozen holes in its crisply uniformed torso.

Silence, except for the hiss and pop of failing circuitry from inside the crashing Semblance-4, and the waterfall barrage of rain on the roof.

"You are unhurt?" Dash Nine inquired.

I'd landed on the couch, a ratty old thing that a generation of bored station monitors had probably done unspeakable things on, and I was happy to clamber off it as soon as I performed a quick physical inventory. There was a tear in one sleeve of my camo jacket, evidence of a bullet's recent passage, but other than that, I'd escaped unharmed.

"Good to go," I said, as I got to my feet. The hamster, remarkably unfazed, reached for another sunflower seed.

Dash Nine clumped over to the wreck of the Semblance-4 and used a front hoof to give it a gentle, almost sympathetic kick to the head. This particular unit had been made to look like a blonde, Caucasian male, lantern-jawed and generically handsome. In general, all robots hold at least some interest for me, but I've never liked Semblance-4s. The flexible polyvinyl and elastomers used to form their skin make them look like ambulatory Barbie dolls. As with Barbies, their eyes blink, but always at the wrong moment. Worst of all are their mouths, because when they talk, you can see they don't have a tongue. The bottom line? Semblance units pretty much define the Uncanny Valley.

"Dysfunctional," Dash said. "This is fortunate. It was one one-hundredth of a millisecond from successfully broadcasting a multi-wavelength distress beacon, which would have taken several minutes to fully scramble."

Now that I wasn't being shot at, or wondering if I'd been hit, my thoughts were racing. This mission had been designed as a relatively low-risk way to test Dash Nine's loyalty, yes, but it was also supposed to be covert. The nominal goal was to add a data miner onto the antennae station's connection feeds, incoming and outgoing both, and to do so in such a way that there was no sign we'd ever been there. Based on past incursions with similar goals, we figured it would take the New Confederation at least a year before routine maintenance discovered that someone (me) had jiggered their system. Instead, the two monitors would be back any minute, caffeinated and cheerful, and they'd walk in to find that their favorite Semblance-4 had got into an all-out fire-fight, a sure sign that they'd been paid a visit by the Free Appalachian Alliance (me again). They'd do three things in quick succession: check the perimeter for hostiles (me, me, me); send a Mayday signal; and start a thorough systems check to see what we'd added, subtracted, or compromised.

So much for stealth, surprise, and subtlety. Stupid Semblance-4. What was it even doing here? They weren't guard-bots. The Semblance line mostly got deployed as cashiers and parking lot attendants, customer service jobs where real people surely had something better to do.

I realized I was staring at the hamster, and it was staring back at me as it fed yet another sunflower seed into its mouth. I heard the tiniest snapping noise at it bit through the shell, and then it got to work, chewing away with busy, squirrel-like intensity. Something about that hamster was starting to bug me, but I couldn't put my finger on it.

"Robin." Dash Nine's voice surprised me; I'd almost forgotten he was there. "Given the altered situation, a full retreat would be the better part of valor."

I leaned close to the aquarium glass, and the hamster, with its beady, jet-black eyes, stared back.

"Earth to Corporal Robin Dell," said Dash, maneuvering itself with difficulty in the cramped room. "'Let's march without the noise of threat'ning drum.'"

That brought me up short. Sad but true: citing obscenely obscure quotes is just about the best way to get my attention. "Dash," I demanded, "what *is* that?"

"Shakespeare. *Richard II.*"

I took a moment to think, partly about King Richard, and partly about the hamster.

"Dash, you did a scan in here for living things. And you said the hamster was alive."

"Which it is."

"Okay, now check for, I don't know, heat emissions. Infra-red."

"Commencing."

With its next seed finished, the hamster tipped its head and gazed at Dash Nine with a questioning, jaunty look, as if challenging my massive killer bot to a wrestling match.

"Remarkable," said Dash Nine, after a moment. "The heat signatures from the hamster's eyes do not match. I must infer that the left eye is robotic."

I scowled. "So, it's recording us. And you haven't been jamming it."

Dash's sleek head nodded gravely. "The hamster is indeed alive, but altered. There is a deformation along its left hip, suggesting an implant, most likely a data storage device. Possibly there is even a data port, but owing to the profusion of fur, I would need to perform a physical exam to be certain. As for jamming, there is no need. The creature's data storage is passive."

"You're sure it's not jacked in?"

"Positive."

Even so, this was rotten news. A hybrid hamster was archiving our every move, leaving me with two choices, both bad. I could take the hamster with us, or smash it under my boot.

"We cannot take it with us," Dash Nine said, once again demonstrating a truly alarming ability to read my thoughts. "Whatever's been done to this hamster, it will continue to record information, and it lacks my sophistication—meaning, it will not play turncoat to its makers and befriend you, as I have. Very likely, it will have been outfitted with an intermittent tracking beacon, one that, until it activates, I will be unable to sense or jam. The safest course of action will be to crush the animal or incinerate it, in hopes of permanently disabling any and all added components."

With my eyes fixed on the orange-yellow hamster, I said nothing.

"Robin. We are on a timetable. We have as little as one minute before the monitors return, and if we wait longer than two minutes, we will likely miss our rendezvous with the extraction team."

No doubt Dash's warnings were sensible, but I was flashing back to my childhood home, where I had once kept a hamster in my bedroom. Mine was a girl, a bit tawnier than the one I faced now, and her smells and scrabblings kept me company from the age of nine until the day I signed up for the resistance, which I did on my fourteenth birthday, the very first day I was eligible. My parents bravely insisted they'd keep Marcia until I returned, but we all knew that was a fantasy. Anyone joining the resistance committed to a minimum ten-year term, and at no point during that tenure would we be permitted contact with anyone from our prior lives, not even parents, siblings, or lovers. The idea was to cut ties, to sever the potential for any critical decisions to be made on the basis of sentiment and emotion. I, and everyone else in the Nest, identified as orphans. Back home, parents and guardians were coached and counseled daily to give up hoping for the best—to treat us as if we were already casualties of war.

And now, here I stood, in an enemy communications bunker, undone by a fur-ball pet that somehow exhibited more mnemonic heft than any novel, movie, or photograph I'd ever encountered. For the first time since my early teens, I suddenly wanted nothing more than to be home, in the arms of my mother, surrounded by our living room's awful orange fleur-de-lis wallpaper, and with my father rushing in from the den, shouting my name in welcome.

"Robin!" Dash Nine's tone had turned urgent. "'Screw your courage to the sticking place!'"

My hesitation was foolish, I knew, and a hamster was a truly maudlin thing to fret over, but I couldn't help it. The damn thing qualified as a civilian, and everything in my training screamed at me to keep civilians from harm.

I'm a freedom fighter, not a terrorist.

"It's a rodent," I said, aloud, as I lost the fight to hold back tears. "It's nothing but a stupid rodent."

Dash Nine nuzzled my shoulder. "And if we do not hurry and end its life, we will be forced to kill two probably harmless, coffee-drinking functionaries. Technicians, not warriors." He paused, as if considering. "If you like, I can do it."

"No."

I reached up, plucked the lid from the aquarium, and tossed it on top of the charred, smoking Semblance-4. Without giving myself time to think, I reached in and seized the hamster with both hands. The idiot creature made no effort to bite or even squirm as I hoisted it free of its glass cage. Stupid thing. Trusting (like me) right to the end.

Hangmen use a rope; headsmen use an axe. If my study of literature had taught me anything at all, it was this: executioners of all stripes rely on tools. And so it was that I gave way to cowardice, and offered the hamster to my robotic partner in crime.

Without comment, Dash Nine reached out with delicate, servo-powered fingers and took the little animal from me. For a moment, nothing happened—the hamster twisted its head around, intent on goodness knows what—and then in a flash, the bot shifted its grip so that it held only the animal's hindquarters, then it brought it down head-first and hard, with brutal force, on the edge of the desk. The chicken-bone crack of its skull made me jump, and I winced so hard I had to shut my eyes.

For a long moment, I simply stood there, frozen, listening to the rain drumming on the blockhouse roof and holding my breath as if I were deep underwater, awaiting some uncertain rescue.I said, almost too quietly to be heard over the rain, "I'd rather kill people."

Dash Nine, with true robotic wisdom, kept his own counsel, and I turned to look him in what might or might not have been his eye. I suspected he actually had several, and those in various locations.

"Dash," I said, "you realize I could never say what I just said in the Nest. Ever."

"Then I am glad that I was the only one to hear it."

"At least with a human being, they've probably done something wrong."

"'Some rise by sin, and some by virtue fall.'"

"Yeah," I said. "That."

With unlooked for sensitivity, Dash Nine deposited the hamster's lifeless body on the floor. "The data card in its hip will hold compromising intel. With your blessing, I will inject concentrated hydrofluoric acid. You do not have to watch."

Shame-faced, I turned away to stare through the exit at the ongoing rainstorm. Behind me, I heard soft clickings and whirrings and a kiss-like sigh of pressurized air. A delivery device of some sort, I decided, presumably not one made of metal, and then my nose quirked as it registered a hot, pungent odor, one I had last experienced in a field ops chemistry lab. I supposed that if I turned around and looked, I'd see a half-liquefied hamster carcass on the concrete floor, its insides bubbling and smoking beneath the remains of its beautiful fur. I told myself that this wasn't my fault, that it was the fault of whatever horrible person had first installed a data device inside the poor animal. I told this to myself several times in quick succession, but I can't say that I was fully convinced.

"Done," said Dash Nine.

"Destroy the CPUs," I said. "Then we go."

Bending low, Dash Nine reached under the table and pulled out the bunker's computer processors, then set to work trampling them. Without looking towards the floor, I smashed the desktop unit, then ripped every data cable I could find from the wall. It wasn't much, not given what we'd come for, just basic vandalism, but at least our various acts of destruction felt cathartic.

Outside, the force of the storm had spent itself, but it was still raining hard enough that I felt certain that we would be impossible to track by any normal means, and sure enough, in less than a minute, as we heard an oncoming vehicle grinding its engine and churning through distant puddles, we were down the ravine and gone, plunging through stands of broad-leafed paw-paw and the occasional screen of young hemlocks. I checked my digital wrist watch, an admittedly old-fashioned affectation, but one I never fail to strap on for field work. According to it, we still had twenty-two minutes to reach our rendezvous point. It had taken us over twenty-six minutes to make the hike in, but we were on a downhill now, and I thought that if we hurried, we might still make it home.

And what would home bring? Vindication, on Jalen Kelsey's part? Not given how today's waterlogged spy-craft had transpired. The lieutenant would question any number of the assumptions I'd made along the way, all tied to claims made by Dash Nine, ones that in the moment I'd accepted as gospel. For example, was it possible that my pet Centaur Seven known all along about the presence of an armed Semblance-4, then failed to inform me, through a simple sin of omission? And what about the now-destroyed hamster? I had only Dash Nine's word that the hamster hadn't been on-line the whole time, in which case, my facial features were now available to a dozen or more New Confed databases, and I would shortly be designated as Public Enemy Number Something-or-Other throughout their territory. For that matter, if I were Lieutenant Kelsey, I'd be thinking that I had no reason beyond a hunch to believe that the hamster was a cyborg in the first place. Even as its body, and all available evidence, was melting away in a hot bath of hydrofluoric, had I seen, with my own eyes, so much as a single prosthetic limb or data port?

No matter how fast I skidded through the leaves and mud, no matter how I concentrated on keeping my balance, these lines of thought refused to give way to something closer to operational terra firma.

In fact, common sense and logic insisted that the lieutenant would be right to harbor these concerns. Dash Nine could be playing the longest of long games. So what if my heart said otherwise? Dash hadn't done anything thus far that expressly endangered a New Confed citizen. It could even be argued that, in hustling me out of the antennae station, he'd been acting to protect the two New Confed station monitors—and wasn't this how I would have run a similar double agent, if I'd managed to insert a clever, adaptable bot into the opposition's covert corps? Were the situation somehow reversed, I, too, would proceed with the longest possible horizon, winning trust with minimal compromise, and only exploding my asset out of sleeper mode when it could do maximum damage. In a clandestine war like ours, was there any other rational course?

Beside me, Dash Nine made yet another accurate guess at my thoughts. "Robin," he said, "assuming we return safely, do you think your comrades at the Nest will now be inclined to trust me?"

The question rankled more than I wanted to admit. "No," I said, "and to do that, we'll have to tackle something really high-stakes, a mission where the likelihood of my being killed is…significant."

Dash Nine, even while splashing through a swampy patch, managed a thoughtful nod. "Your cohorts have lost friends to Centaur Sevens."

"Exactly. And overcoming that level of distrust…"

In a voice of surrender, my bot said, "The Leinster Conundrum remains unsolved. I must be seen to pick sides. Irrevocably."

The rain had slowed to a trickle. Through a scrim of rising mist and damp, glossy tree trunks, a strip of gravel road came into view, and on it, pulling to a gentle stop, was a plain white cargo van: the Nest's extraction team, our ticket home. Perfect timing.

Was it a coincidence that at the same moment that I spotted the van, I had an epiphany?

"Dash," I said, "in concrete terms, what we need to do—"

"—is put me in a position where I must protect you with lethal force against my former New Confed controllers. Only then will your venerated Lieutenant Kelsey learn sufficient faith in my newfound loyalties."

I nodded. "Bingo. With a double dose of bing."

It's funny how the past never quite prepares you for the U-turns of the future. I accept and even embrace a life of calculated risk, but under normal circumstances, I would never have intentionally selected any mission where I was likely to be discovered, outed, shot at—killed—but the advent of Dash Nine had upended all my past protocols, just as I'd upended his. As things now stood, only the diciest, most aggressive choices were worth making.

But not today. The remainder of this day would be about a quick run back to the Nest, followed by a debrief and a scalding hot shower. After that, over the next days or weeks, there would be ample time to cook up the most outrageous cross-border mission in the Nest's necessarily underground and as yet unwritten history.

"'Once more,'" said Dash Nine, as we arrived at the roadside embankment, and checked both ways for prying eyes. "'Once more into the breach.'"

"Or the van," I suggested, as I clambered up the bank and in through the sliding side door.

"'Dear friends,'" added Dash. "Let us never forget our friends."

"Never," I said, as Dash Nine squeezed in beside me, and I gave his alloy flanks a friendly pat. But even as the van door slid shut, even as I gave our driver the okay to make for the relative safety of home, I couldn't help dredging up O. Henry's paranoid aphorism, "No friendship is an accident." If that were true, then friendship implied enemy action.

Gravel crunched under the van's tires as we pulled away, and the sound made me think of tiny bones, breaking.

Homeward bound.

This Ends Part II of *Taming Dash Nine*

Mark Rigney has had over fifty short pieces find print in a gentle arc covering the last two decades, with stories in Lightspeed, Realms of Fantasy, and more. Theatrical credits, too, with play across the U.S., including off-Broadway, along with Canada, Hong Kong, Nepal, and Australia.

Big Screen Little Screen

Mark Bilsborough

I was going to open this column by saying we truly live in a golden age of onscreen speculative fiction, but then I realised we don't. Sure, the production values are great, the writing sometimes borders on outstanding and there are some genuinely superlative moments. But widescreen 4D with top-end surround sound is only fantastic if you can afford it and there's still not much on at the movies, post-Covid.

Plus (and this is really a big minus) although we've been promised it for years, we've got no new *Stargate* and no new *Battlestar Galactica*. Hell, we haven't even got any more *Firefly* and that's been decades. *The Expanse* has been cancelled (again, and please tell me it's not permanent this time), *Doctor Who* seems to drip new episodes out once a century or so and Paramount, in its infinite wisdom, decided to pull *Star Trek Discovery* from UK schedules right before it was due to be released so it can head up yet another paid streaming service that has *no firm UK release date*. All I can say is thank the gods for *Picard*.

Ah, *Picard*. Patrick Stewart has always looked old, but now he genuinely is so don't expect an extended run of this fine series (scheduled to end after season 3). Fortunately there's a great supporting cast surrounding him, including the inestimable Seven of Nine (Jeri Ryan) and a Borg queen so chilling it's a wonder anyone would take her on a jaunt back to the 20th century, you know, just in case. This cast could surely sustain a series or two on its own, so the future here looks bright and leaves me hungry for *Star Trek: Strange New Worlds*, out in May (assuming Paramount will let us see it).

Marvel keeps churning stuff out, too, and they're deftly sidestepping creative dead ends, at least in the TV versions. Recent outings for *Loki* and *Hawkeye* have been excellent and have had lasting impacts on the characters and (in Loki's case) the Marvel Cinematic Universe as a whole. The latest offering is *Moon Knight*, which is a first outing for this (relatively) minor Marvel character. He's American mercenary Marc

Spector, who transforms into the muscle (or fist') for Egyptian god Khonshu He also transforms, inconveniently, into gift shop nerd Steven Grant, because he's (they've) got something called dissociative identity disorder. The whole series is relocated from the comics to London and it feels very British, though the cast is diverse and international. Moon Knight is edgy and complex, sometimes funny and always entertaining. The Moon Knight costume is effective and the narrative sits just the right side of bloody confusing.

Nothing's really new though, just developments on themes. That's as true of *Moon Knight* (in the comics since 1975) as it is of *Picard* (on TV since 1987). And it's true, too of Boba Fett, the titular hero of *The Book of Boba Fett*, now on Disney+. It's the latest in the Star Wars extended universe, following on from the wildly successful *Mandalorian*. Fett first appeared in the *Star Wars Holiday Special* in 1978 (best forgotten) but had extensive roles in both 1980's *Empire Strikes Back* and *1983's Return of the Jedi* and in various places after. Fett's a bounty hunter back on legendary sandy planet Tattooine trying to claim Jabba the Hut's old territory. It's entertaining, but don't expect major developments and it's garnered indifferent reviews. Maybe it's hard to be original with such a well established franchise, particularly for a series infilling in the wider story arc. We've got Obi Wan Kenobi coming up, with the return of Euan MacGregor. Expect no surprises.

We've also recently had the third series of *Snowpiercer* (excellent, but seen first on screen in a 2013 movie), a new series, *Peacemaker* (seen before in Suicide Squad) and more Titans (increasingly violent and foul-mouthed), *the Witcher* (entertaining but not exactly new), *The Last Kingdom* (third and final outing) and *Raised by Wolves* (unnervingly excellent and growing into its second season) And, of course, a new take on *The Batman*.

Just to reinforce the seen it all before theme this is going to be the year of prequels. We're getting a *Witcher* prequel series, *A Lord of the Rings* series set way before the events of the books and a *Game of Thrones* prequel. Plus *Foundation* on Apple and another version of *Dune* in the movies. Ah, nostalgia.

But there is originality out there. *Upload* is now on its second season and still breaking new (comedic) ground, following Nathan, uploaded to a virtual retirement village on his untimely (and deliberate) death and Ben Stiller's *Severance*, where memories of the working day are forgotten at home (and vice versa) due to nifty mind altering tech. But there's conspiracy afoot, and the characters' maddening inability to remember what goes on at home when they're at work (and vice versa) makes for a strange, tense and competing narrative.

So some hope but mainly rehashes. All we need now is a new *Jurassic Park* movie and the nostalgia fest will be complete. Wait a sec…

Bookworm

Sandra Davies Baker

The Infernal Riddle of Thomas Peach
by Jas Treadwell

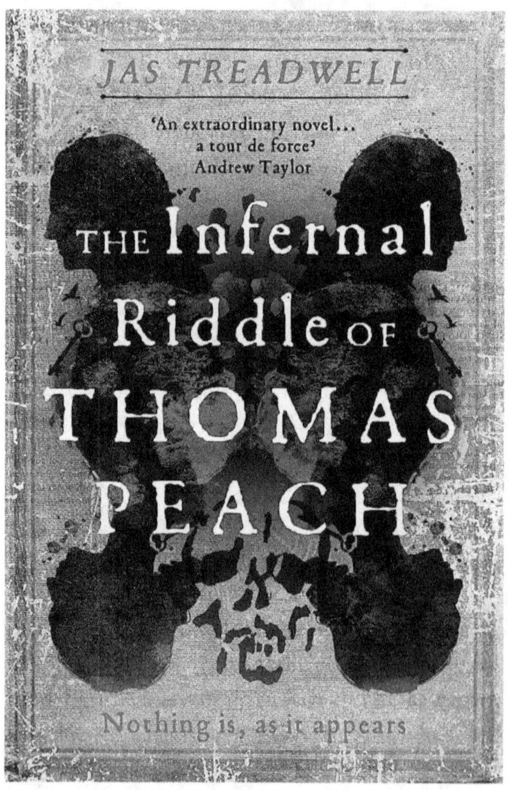

"Ah reader – what mysteries you shall compel us to expose! Will you step but a little further into the churchyard?" From the gold embossed cover of the book, with its 18th Century typeface, to the quaint writing style and use of footnotes, Jas Treadwell has worked hard to create an authentic feel to his tale of Thomas Peach, a gentleman of *'modest means'*.

From the start, the narrator sounds like a collective – *"We transport you to the year seventeen eighty five."* There is a distance between the storyteller(s) and the reader from the start, often the former consulting the latter directly as to what they might think or feel about the notorious events that happen. This successfully creates the atmosphere of an 18th Century novel, but it often stands in the way of a total engagement with the story.

So, to the plot. Thomas Peach moves to a remote corner of Somerset in 1785 to nurse his ailing wife. But his wife is never seen, and gossip soon spreads around the village. Peach is a member of a society of learned men in Bristol, one of whom is guardian of a young woman believed to be possessed by a demon. In one particularly chilling scene, this woman turns to Peach to reveal that her mouth and lips are inexplicably stained a deep, dark black.

Their paths become disturbingly entangled and Peach soon begins to suspect that in her past lies a dreadful secret . . .

A gothic novel utilising 21st Century writing skills, 'The Infernal Riddle' is a challenging read. It is basically one long, slow reveal, using beautifully crafted language and contextual references. That said, it is also entertaining, often amusing and definitely intriguing. I particularly liked the way I became totally immersed in this 18th century world – the author's attention to tone and detail is impressive.

And so, to the author. 'Jas Treadwell' is a pseudonym, described in the flyleaf as: *"A phantom – a cipher – A mere name, assumed like a mask! and signifying, nothing at all."*

Rumour has it, 'Jas Treadwell' is an author previously published under another name but whose identity is being kept anonymous for this book. So, dear reader, shall we surmise that he or she is *"of no importance, nor significance to any person in all the world,"* as Thomas Peach describes himself. Or ...?

The Ninth Metal
By Benjamin Percy

It begins with a comet and the action is pretty much nonstop from there on, in this fast-paced novel by Benjamin Percy. The premise is that while the earth breathes a sigh of relief when a huge comet doesn't crash into it, the world hadn't allowed for the subsequent meteor shower created by the falling debris. It's a big, big meteor shower and it has massive consequences – which are life-changing, but not in terms of an extinction event. More in terms of revealing the greed, corruption and power games created by the discovery of precious metals from outer space.

'The Ninth Metal' reads likes Stephen King, mixed with Lee Child with a dash of Marvel's 'Jennifer Jones'. I couldn't put it down, it felt like being in the cinema or binge watching a box set. Percy has King's ability to instantly create realistic, three-dimensional characters and then use their points of view to run the narrative. The action scenes are intense, and the descriptive passages are well observed – it's no surprise to learn that Percy writes comics for Marvel and DC.

The narrative jumps around in time, revealing the characters' worlds before, during and after the meteor shower. The precious metal left by the shower (arriving in dramatic, crater inducing fashion) is named 'Omnimetal'. It offers humankind huge possibilities, but it has to be mined from the earth. A kind of modern day mining goldrush ensues, with disputes over land and ownership. To add to the dystopian plot, 'Omnimetal' can also be used as a drug, which is consumed in great quantities by 'metal-eaters', whose bright blue eyes reveal their addiction.

The protagonist – John Frontier – returns to his hometown of Northfall, Minnesota after a long absence, only to be taken aback to see how the town has changed since the discovery of Omnimetal deposits. His story is one of self-discovery, family secrets, loyalty, and loss. His family basically run the town, except now, with the arrival of Omnimetal, they have competition. The kind of competition that will kill for power and profit.

Gripping as the narrative may be, there are a few too many loose ends and underexplored ideas that get in the way. For example, the suggestion of an alien connection with Omnimetal isn't fully developed – where did the comet come from? Why and how is this new metal so powerful? How and why does it give humans special powers? 'The Ninth Metal' is apparently the first of a cycle of novels from Percy that is set in a shared universe. It feels like the author has deliberately not developed certain ideas with this cycle in mind. I found this frustrating, and I felt a bit cheated out of knowing more.

That said, if 'The Ninth Metal' is an indication of the quality of things to come, I'll definitely be reading the next in the series. Highly recommended.

A Desolation Called Peace
By Arkady Martine

Oh, this is good. *Award winningly* good, if there's any justice. It's the follow up to 2019's A *Memory Called Empire* and continues the story of the compromised and complicated Lsel Ambassador to the mighty Teixcallani Empire as she navigates impossible politics to try and avert an intergalactic conflict, faced by enemies she can barely comprehend, let alone communicate with.

This is layered science fiction with complex, overlapping points of view set in the far future (or distant past – the narrative is entirely without reference to our own history). It leads directly from its predecessor novel, where tensions between Lsel and the Empire are kept at an uneasy arms length in the face of an incipient alien threat, and which follows Mahit Dzmore (the new Lsel Ambassador) as she negotiates her way though her new posting, where she's considered a barbarian, and her own mind, which is stuffed with the thoughts of two iterations of her predecessor, due to her being fitted with an 'imago', which carries

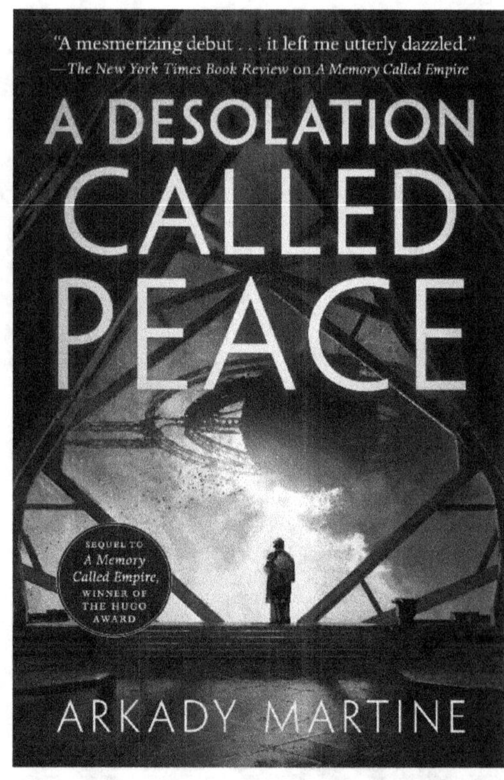

memory (an consciousness) of the dead to the living.

In this new novel, the alien threat is becoming more tangible. New Empire colonies are being attacked by enemy ships with superior firepower. One colony is completely destroyed, and all its inhabitants brutally eviscerated. Within the Empire there are factions that want war, and factions that want peace and this is played out in the tension between Nine Hibiscus, the leader of the fleet (who wants to negotiate), and one of her uppity captains, Sixteen Moonrise (who wants to attack)

In the middle of this is Three Seagrass, an information officer tasked with leading the negotiations, and Mahit Dzmore, who she drags along to help. The stakes are high – and as the novel builds, so does the tension.

One thing this novel does well is convey the utter *alienness* of the (unnamed) aliens, and understanding how that motivates them is an important part of the negotiations. Another is the characterisation: the author gives us multiple perspectives and yet creates some distinct, full and memorable characters. We've got the Empress, fighting off discordant voices in the Ministry of War, and the heir, the eleven year old Eight Antidote, with his refreshing insights and his determination to do what's right. Then there's Mahit Dzmore and her various enemies both in Lsel Station and the Empire, quick witted and impulsive, but faced with an impossible choice, and her putative love interest, Three Seagrass, who is strongly drawn to her barbarian friend but who feels that she'll invariably say the wrong thing and drive her lover away, And, finally, the fleet captain, Nine Hibiscus, fighting off treachery within and danger without, and her loyal adjutant Twenty Cicadia.

That's a lot of perspectives to cram into one novel (and there are others – the aliens, for instance, with interlude passages which I suspect are deliberately incomprehensible just to make the point that these are *aliens*. And because of that, early on this story is difficult to engage with. It's probably easier if read immediately after *A Memory Called Empire* but otherwise it takes a while to get into the odd naming structures and the byzantine politics of the Empire and Lsel Station. But there's a point – about a hundred pages in – when this story starts to fly and it's worth all the head scratching and back-referring to get to that point.

Everyone in the Empire has a name beginning with a number (though I do wish the old emperor hadn't been called Six Direction), which differentiates them from the barbarians on Lsel Station who have names which feel like jumbled sets of letters – hard to like, hard to recall. It all emphasises we're a long way from our reality, though the sheer proliferation of characters with odd names makes it hard to follow the storyline, particularly early on.

But that's a minor quibble. This is the best book I've read for a long time and thoroughly deserves all the plaudits it will undoubtedly get. *(MB)*

Wyldblood Magazine #8, Spring 2022.
© 2022 Wyldblood Press and contributors.

Publisher: Wyldblood Press, Thicket View, Bakers Lane, Maidenhead SL6 6PX UK. www.wyldblood.com **Editor:** Mark Bilsborough. **Fiction editor** Sandra Baker. **First readers:** Vaughan Stanger, Mike Lewis, Rebecca Ruvinsky, Bailey Spencer.
Subscriptions: 4 issues epub/mobi/pdf delivered to your inbox £11. 4 issue print subscriptions £22.
www.wyldblood.com/magazine Single issues available worldwide via Amazon and from Wyldblood:

Submissions: we are regularly open for submissions of flash fiction, short stories and novels – check our website for our current status and requirements. We are a paying market. We also need artwork, people to review us, and people to review *for* us. Email contact@wyldblood.com

ISBN 978-1-914417-09-2